dark, funny, and scary! That's the way I like my women. But
…cription also fits this delightfully appalling look at Hollywood.
… and be glad all this stuff isn't happening to you'
Harry Shearer of *This is Spinal Tap* and *The Simpsons*

…e again pulls off a cunning narrative trick. Our gratitude at being
…nside a glamorous showbiz world is constantly matched by our
…ude that we don't have to live there. Long's writing always has a
…ouch and plenty of good jokes. Even so, this doesn't prevent him
…providing a dark picture of Hollywood – where talent is regarded
…ly as a threat to the untalented, and the only sure way to get approval
…undergo some personal tragedy' James Walton, *Sunday Telegraph*

…rious, frank and very addictive'   *Daily Mail*

…novel within a novel within a script is an hilarious, shocking and
…st account of how Hollywood really works'   *Daily Mirror*

…of witty asides, Long's book explains the importance of distinguishing
…een a complimentary fruit basket (sent by management out of
…ne appreciation) and a fruit basket "with subtext" (ie which
…ates that your show's been canned). A funny guide to a world
…cumlocutory madness'   Christopher Silvester, *Sunday Times*

…very funny . . . as riveting and real as gossip. Indeed, there's a
…nt section on the nature and meaning of Hollywood gossip . . .
…'s just enough moral weight in this hugely enjoyable book to make
…wonder if it's all really worth it' Frank Cottrell Boyce, *Guardian*

…ook of the year . . . This book is a wonderfully heretical account
…s career as a sitcom producer. There's simply no more reliable
…e to contemporary Hollywood'
Toby Young, *Evening Standard* Books of the Year

'The funniest and wisest thing to come out of Tinseltown since *Curb
Your Enthusiasm*'   *Arena*

BY THE SAME AUTHOR

Conversations with My Agent

SET UP, JOKE, SET UP, JOKE

ROB LONG

BLOOMSBURY

First published in Great Britain in 2005

This paperback edition published 2007

Copyright © 2005 by Rob Long

The moral right of the author has been asserted

Bloomsbury Publishing Plc, 36 Soho Square, London W1D 3QY

Bloomsbury Publishing, London, New York and Berlin

A CIP catalogue record for this book is available from the British Library

ISBN 9780747579694

10 9 8 7 6 5 4 3 2 1

Typeset by Palimpsest Book Production Limited, Grangemouth, Stirlingshire
Printed in Great Britain by Clays Ltd, St Ives plc

All papers used by Bloomsbury Publishing are natural, recyclable products
made from wood grown in well-managed forests. The manufacturing
processes conform to the environmental regulations of the country of origin

www.bloomsbury.com

To
TRF
And the F. family

This book is half true.

CONTENTS

The First Meeting, Monday Morning, 10:30 AM

'Hi.'

'Hi.'

'We'll be right with you. Did someone offer you coffee?'

'Yeah, I think it's coming.'

'Great, great. Well. Anyway. They'll be right with you. I'm sorry it's taken so long. But it's a conference call, so . . .'

'Right, right.'

'I'm Josh, by the way. I'm new in the comedy development department.'

'Oh, great. Nice to meet you, Josh. But, wait a minute . . . wasn't the guy before you . . .'

'Also named Josh? Yeah.'

'And where did he go?'

'Nowhere. He's my boss.'

'Oh.'

'That's Josh now. He's waving us in.'

'Okay, then.'

'Don't forget your coffee.'

'Hi!'

'Hi!'

'Hi!'

'Hi!'

'Hi!'

'Hi!'

'This is Josh, and you've met Josh, and this is Trish and Trish's assistant Tori, and Eli and Beth and Jamal.'

'Hi, Josh, and Trish, and Tori and Eli and Beth and . . . I'm sorry . . .'

'Jamal.'

'Jamal, right, right. Sorry.'

'Don't be sorry!'

'Josh still hasn't learned our names. And he's the boss!'

'So I heard. Congratulations, Josh.'

'I'm Eli.'

'Maybe it'd be easier for me if you all wore name tags.'

'Hahahahahahaha.'

'Hahahahahahaha.'

'Hahahahahahaha.'

'Funny! You're a funny guy. So why don't you tell us what you've got today?'

'Great. Great. See, I was thinking about something—'

'Can I interrupt you for a moment?'

'Of course, Josh.'

'I just want to say how much I've loved your work and how really grateful I am that you're here today.'

'Me too.'

'Me too.'

'Gosh, thanks, Josh and ... Eli and ... Trish and ... all of you.'

'Big fan.'

'Thanks.'

'So, sorry, continue.'

'Well, what I was going to say was that one of the things that I've been thinking about is how, well, how mysterious all of this ... business, this television producing business, is to most people, and I was thinking about some kind of ... I don't know ... kind of half-comic half-tragic look at this business through the eyes of a writer, maybe a guy like me.'

'Yeah.'

'Okay.'

'Let's think about this for a minute.'

'I agree with Josh.'

'Me too.'

'Well, okay, I was thinking it could be in, like, a pastiche of forms – maybe part of it will be in screenplay format, maybe part of it will be in the form of stories and anecdotes – I mean, you guys know how much people in this town like to sit around and gossip and tell war stories, right? – and that maybe it'll form some kind of accurate picture or snapshot – kind of an impressionistic thing, I guess – about the inner workings of and the state of our business. I mean, not this – I'm just throwing this out – but what if the spine of the story was, like, the life cycle of one television series?'

'Hmmmm.'
'Hmmmm.'
'Hmmmm.'
'Hmmmm.'
'I love it.'
'I agree with Josh.'
'I do too.'
'Me too.'
'The only thing I'm not crazy about is that it's about the television business and that it's about you.'
'But does it have to be about the television business?'
'I think Trish raises an interesting point. Does it?'
'And does it have to be about you?'
'Does it?'
'Does it?'
'I ... well ... I mean, it's ...'
'Doesn't matter, really. Let's try it. Let's see how it goes. Let's play around with the area and see what happens. Is that okay?'
'Can we play around with the area?'
'I love the area.'
'It's a great area.'
'It's a really interesting area to play with.'
'So let's play with it.'
'Okay?'
'Okay?'
'Okay?'

4

SPRING: 'ON THE BUBBLE'

FADE IN:
A famous actor once tried to describe the rigors of being in production. The hours are long, the food is mediocre, the living quarters are cramped. 'Basically,' he said, without a smidgen of irony, 'it's like Auschwitz.'

Of course, a holocaust is in the eyes of the beholder, and for him I guess hell was a double-wide trailer and three catered meals a day. For the rest of us, though, being in production is *not at all* like Auschwitz. It's not even like taking the *tour* of Auschwitz. It's not even, at its worst, like taking a trip to Poland. The only thing even remotely similar between those two things is that in each case, one's first impulse is to hide in the attic.

We have just finished producing twenty-two episodes of a half-hour television series. We are *on hiatus*, as the lingo goes. If your show is a hit – or even, in these days of diminished expectations, a moderate success – the concept of a *hiatus* is identical to the concept of a 'holiday.' Your show is definitely going to be on the network's fall schedule and you have about eight weeks to relax and go to Hawaii. If your show is not a hit – that is to say, if your show is written and produced by me – the concept of *hiatus* is closer to the concept of *frantic period of intense speculation and worry*. The production schedule of a normal twenty-two-episode season ends around the first week in March. The networks make their decisions about which shows to keep and which shows to drop in the middle of May. You see the problem here? Two-and-a-half months of speculation.

Our sitcom premiered to generally good reviews – some outright raves, from influential critics in the *Los Angeles Times*, *New York Newsday*, and *Media Week* – and low but not shabby ratings. Our situation, though, in the last four weeks before the networks announce their new schedules, is precarious. Because we cannot claim to be an outright ratings success, and because the network on which our show appears requires, above all, an outright ratings success, the word on our show is murky. *Variety*, the entertainment industry trade paper, has more or less written us off as a 'promising rookie' that has had trouble 'delivering'. I have been in the television business for six years and I am still waiting to attain the necessary diffidence to be able to read things about myself in *Variety* without lapsing into a kind of enraged hyperventilation.

CUT TO:
INT. MY OFFICE – DAY
I am at my desk smoking a cigar. That afternoon our

office received a strongly-worded memo reminding us that California state law prohibits smoking in office buildings.

SFX: phone rings. It's my agent.

    ME

        What have you heard?

    MY AGENT (V.O.)

        Okay. No pleasantries, I guess. Hi. How are you? I'm fine, thanks. Me too. Not bad weather we're having. I agree, it's very pleasant. Especially in the evenings. Yes, they're very—

    ME

        I'm sorry. I guess I'm just a little tense. The waiting.

    MY AGENT (V.O.)

        I understand. It's a complicated time. Have you heard anything from the network?

    ME

        I haven't heard much. The numbers were pretty good – we're 'trended up,' the studio says. We did better than the show that had our time slot before us. The reviews have been gratifying. All in all, I'd say we're in good shape to get on the fall schedule.

    MY AGENT (V.O.)

        Oh. Gosh. I was hoping you were going to say that the ratings were sluggish and dis-appointing, that the network had higher

7

expectations, and that you're a long shot for
fall.

ME

Why were you hoping I'd say that?

MY AGENT (V.O.)

Because it's the truth. And I wasn't in the
mood to deliver bad news.

ME

Um . . .

MY AGENT (V.O.)

It just brings the whole day down, you know?

ME

Yes, I suppose I can see how it would.

MY AGENT (V.O.)

Look, you're on the bubble, what can I say?

ME

Nothing, I guess.

CUT TO:

Our show is *on the bubble*, which is an industry term
I've never really understood. *Bubbles* are fun, gassy things
– they bring to mind balloons, champagne, celebrations.
Yet to be *on the bubble* – which sounds like a Bertie
Woosterism for *a little bit tipsy* – is to be neither officially
cancelled nor officially picked up. It means they're still
trying to decide about you. Still trying to figure out
whether to order your show for one more year and give
you a shot at the apartment in Paris, or dredge up a sad-
sounding voice and get their assistant to track you down.

What you do know, though, is this: the official call, when it comes, will come at the last legal minute. You also know this: the official call, when it comes, will come about five or six days *after* you've already heard, from agents, studio executives, and, probably, the girl at Peet's Coffee. And you also know this: there really is no *on the bubble*; uncertainty is just bad news that's taking its time. If you're a hit – and to get a second season these days, you must be at least someone's definition of a hit – you know it. And if you don't know it, well, there's a reason for that.

If there is one rock-solid axiom in this business – maybe in every business, I don't know – it's that when you hear the rumor of bad news about your show, your money, your career, your livelihood, that rumor is always true. *Always.* At the risk of inciting legal action from certain major celebrities who have battled certain major rumors for years, let me stick my neck out further: those rumors are true, too. Or true enough. Essentially true.

This is, after all, the least imaginative place on earth. This is where people agree to spend hundreds of millions of dollars on movies because they remind them of other movies that have already been made. This is where old sitcoms are turned into either big budget feature films or low budget reality television shows. Do you really think people have the inclination or the imagination to *invent* rumors out of whole cloth? Of course not.

When you hear that your show is being cancelled and replaced with *Candid Camera Uncensored!* it may in fact turn out to be cancelled for *Family Candid Camera* or

Kids 'n' Candid Camera or even something completely different. But it is going to be cancelled. The essence of the rumor is true. And the truth hurts. That's how you can tell it's the truth.

CUT TO:

EXT. SANTA MONICA STREET – DAY

I am wandering around in the middle of the day, walking the dog. I bump into a friend. She looks at me for a long time with a sad and confused expression.

> FRIEND
>
> Hi?
>
> ME
>
> Oh hi. How are you?
>
> FRIEND
>
> (disconcerted)
>
> Fine. And how about you? Are you okay? Is everything . . . okay?
>
> ME
>
> Yeah.
>
> FRIEND
>
> You look . . . different.
>
> ME
>
> Oh, yeah, well I haven't shaved in a few days.
>
> FRIEND
>
> And tired.
>
> ME
>
> Yeah, well, we just finished twenty-two episodes, so I guess I am a little tired.

FRIEND
   And you've gained weight.
ME
   Well, see you around.

CUT TO:
Of course, she's right: I do look tired and I have gained weight. Unfortunately, the solutions to those two problems are mutually exclusive, so I have elected to remain tired for a few weeks while I try to work off the twenty-two episodes I have gained since the start of production. I have a writer friend who claims to own a pair of 'hiatus alarm trousers.' When he must lie down to button them, it's time to go on hiatus.

CUT TO:
EXT. SAN VICENTE BLVD – DAY
I'm driving to the gym. The phone rings.
   MY AGENT (V.O.)
      I ran into the head of the network at lunch.
   ME
      And?
   MY AGENT (V.O.)
      You don't want to know where?
   ME
      No.
   MY AGENT (V.O.)
      The Grill. He was at The Grill.

ME

And?

MY AGENT (V.O.)

We had a conversation about the show.
And his tone was interesting.

ME

What was his tone?

MY AGENT (V.O.)

In a word, *elegiac*. His tone was *elegiac*. Some,
with a smaller vocabulary and a lack of appreciation for nuance, which is not something I
do not have, might say *funereal*. But I think
elegiac conveys the proper ambiguity.

ME

Actually, it doesn't sound all that ambiguous.

MY AGENT (V.O.)

Meaning?

ME

Meaning, it sounds like we're dead. I wish
somebody would just call me up and tell me
that, straight out. Just say, 'Sorry, didn't work,
we're cancelling the show,' rather than all of
this . . . this mystery.

MY AGENT (V.O.)

Not following you.

ME

Why can't they just say it now? Why do they
have to wait until May?

>   MY AGENT (V.O.)
>   Because May is when they announce.
>   ME
>   Why can't they announce *now*?
>   MY AGENT (V.O.)
>   Because it's not May.
>   ME
>   Yeah, but—
>   MY AGENT (V.O.)
>   You're breaking up. Hello? I think I lost you?
>   Hello? Can you hear me? Can you hear me
>   now?

CUT TO:

Our show started strong. We premiered to good numbers, held a respectable slice of the previous show's audience, and in general behaved in a fashion that could best be called 'diligent.'

But these days, ratings described as 'diligent' and 'solid' are not enough to keep a show on the air. The stakes are simply too high. To stay on the air these days, a show must either show ratings growth, or be owned by the network on which it airs. Our show can boast neither. The weird thing is, these days a show garnering a 12 or 13 per cent ratings share can be considered a hit. Five years ago, it would have been yanked during the first commercial break. Our show delivered what will, in a few years, be considered stellar smash-hit numbers. The problem is, it's not a few years from now, it's now. We're ahead of the curve.

CUT TO:

INT. CITRUS RESTAURANT – DAY

I have cleaned myself up for a business lunch (dry salad, grilled fish, fizzy water) with a network executive. Although the network won't announce their fall schedule for four more weeks, I am consumed with curiosity about the fate of our program. The wisest thing would be to simply decline the invitation and pretend to be out of town – after all, the decision is out of my hands completely and I'll just drive myself crazy trying to work the various angles. But since I'm not out of town and I've shaved and taken off about seven episodes so far, I go – vowing to play it cool.

ME

So, are we cancelled or what? Just tell me.

NETWORK EXECUTIVE

Well, you're not cancelled.

ME

We're not?

NETWORK EXEC

Not so far. But it's early still. We haven't even screened some of the new pilots we're considering for next fall.

ME

What if those all turn out great?

NETWORK EXEC

C'mon! You know that never happens. We develop thirty scripts and shoot about ten pilots. We're lucky to get two or three that have potential.

ME
　Oh.
NETWORK EXEC
　It's a great show. You guys have done a ter-
　rific show. Everybody at the network loves it.
ME
　But?
A long pause.
NETWORK EXEC
　It's complicated.
ME
　Complicated how?
NETWORK EXEC
　Let's just leave it at 'it's complicated.' (then,
　brightly) So, any big hiatus plans? You look
　great, by the way. Have you lost weight?

CUT TO:
In Hollywood, when things are described as 'complicated,'
the news is rarely good. Tumors and cancerous lesions
are 'complicated.' Mega-hits and sure things are simple.
Big fat checks are simpler still.

　What's complicated, in a town like this one, is that
information is rarely informative. In the weeks between
March and May, so much gossip is tossed back and forth,
so many projects are *sure things* on Monday that become
dead on arrival by Thursday, that the best, sanest, course
of action is to muffle out all the noise altogether.

　Still, the great thing about rumors is that there's always

one to hang on to. For the ninety-nine pieces of nega-tive information you hear about your project, there's always at least one more that you can embroider and inflate in your mind that means, *We're a sure thing for the fall schedule. I heard it from a guy who was in the meeting.*

Also: gossip, when it's about other people and their troubles, is fun.

For instance, here is the latest, hottest, most impossible-to-substantiate rumor racing through town:

A hugely rich media mogul and his wife engage in a kinky three-way involving bondage, light sadism, and a young lady from Thailand. In an act of monumental fool-ishness – almost biblical in its irony – the mogul video-tapes the entire session (dirty talk, leather masks, *everything*) forgetting that these days everything that's recorded eventually finds its way into the hands of the press.

Call it 'Flynt's Law,' named for Larry Flynt, publisher of every fifteen-year-old boy's favorite read, *Hustler*. Any humiliating act, caught on film, audio- or videotape will be revealed, like water seeking its level, in the most excru-ciatingly painful way. If you cheat on your wife, she will not receive the incriminating photographs in a scruffy envelope in private. She will see them in a newspaper brought to her attention by your children. If you confess strange passions to a good friend in a neighborhood bar, the audiotape will be played coast-to-coast and your mother will hear it first.

The rumor continues: somehow, the video cassette slips out of the mogul's house (they have a way of doing this) and into the hands of one of America's most notorious pornographers. This is hot stuff, he thinks to himself, and prepares to publish stills from the videotape in a multi-part, multi-issue format entitled, no doubt, *A Hollywood Sextravaganza!*

Faced with the kind of embarrassment that would make anyone – even a billionaire media mogul – want to crawl up his own ass, the mogul makes a final, desperate plea. He calls the pornographer up and begs – *begs* – him not to publish the photographs. The two men are, he says, in essentially the same business. They have, he says, many things in common. There is, he declares, no end to the respect and esteem which he, billionaire media mogul, has for the man who made a hundred million dollars selling what are essentially gynecological illustrations.

The pornographer relents. He promises not to print the photographs and has the original video cassette messengered back to the mogul's office. He makes a few copies for private viewing, of course. Or so goes the rumor.

CUT TO:
INT. AOC RESTAURANT – NIGHT
I am out to dinner with an old friend. She is a reporter for a couple of national publications, and has developed what the colorful phrasemakers out here call 'a brand identity.' She is known as an excellent journalist, a witty writer, and, best of all, someone with the ability to explain

this confusing city to the rest of the country, or, at least, to New York. In her latest column, she refers knowingly to the rumor about the media mogul and the pornographer, claiming to have seen the tape herself and recognized the mogul's 'distinctive voice.' But she doesn't name names. So I have invited her out to a swish dinner for the sole purpose of finding out who it is. From the first drink to the salad course, I feign interest in her career. Over the fish, I ask thoughtful questions about her child. Then, finally, over dessert, I pounce.

ME

Tell me who it is.

MY FRIEND

I can't. I'm sworn to secrecy.

For some reason, I'm unable to accept this. It's as if, faced with a career in an industry that renders me powerless – tossed around by the whims of actors, executives, marketing guys, and, ultimately, one hundred million distracted television viewers – I *need* to know which mogul did what to whom and with what in his mouth when he did it. I've been at the mercy of rumor-mongers and gossips for months – '*You're show is looking great!*' '*Your show is history!*' – so I need something to chew on that involves somebody else's ass. Literally, in this case.

ME

Tell me! Tell me tell me tell me tell me!

She looks at me brimming with pity. She closes her eyes and sighs.

MY FRIEND

    You're pathetic.

ME

    I'm a writer in Hollywood. How is this news?

She takes a sip of her wine, looks around the restaurant furtively, and then:

MY FRIEND

    Okay. Okay. I'll tell you. But you have to promise me that you won't tell anyone who it is.

ME

    I won't. Tellmetellmetellme.

MY FRIEND

    Because this guy is *very* powerful. This isn't just some Hollywood rumor, okay? This is BIG stuff. I could lose my job over this.

ME

    I understand.

I try hard to shrug nonchalantly.

ME (CONT'D)

    Tellmetellmetellme.

She leans forward, and then in a voice barely audible, low and sad, she tells me the name of the mogul who taped his three-way and begged the pornographer and barely missed being flattened by the giant anvil of shame, humiliation, and embarrassment that hovers above us all, suspended by the slenderest thread imaginable, ready for Flynt's Law to bring it crashing down.

    And let me tell you, it's one big fat juicy name. I mean,

wow! I only wish I could tell you who it is. Can't though. You'll just have to guess.

Let me tell you another story that's making the rounds in Hollywood. It's a 'salad course' story – it lasts just long enough to finish a salad at lunch, and is flexible enough to segue easily to the 'main course' story, which lasts a little longer, until the 'decaf cappuccino' portion of the lunch, which is when we get down to business.

A young actor discovers that his girlfriend – with whom he thought he had an exclusive arrangement – is seeing another guy on the side. He learns the identity of this 'sloppy seconds' character – an agent's assistant at a powerful agency – and heads over to his place of work for a man-to-man chat. Once in the agency lobby, he belligerently demands that the assistant come down and face him. Finally, the assistant appears, all 6 feet, 190 muscled pounds of him. The actor gets his ass kicked all over the lobby. The assistant gets promoted, because his bosses are agents, and all agents secretly hate all actors.

CUT TO:
INT. MY OFFICE – DAY
I am on the phone with an acquaintance, a notorious gossip who prides himself on knowing everything first. He has just told me that the president of one of the large television networks is about to be fired.

MY FRIEND (V.O.)
Got anything for me?

ME
>   Nope, sorry. We've been in production on our
>   series for the past year, so I'm sort of out of
>   the loop.

MY FRIEND (V.O.)
>   (disappointed)
>   Oh. But I just gave you a really juicy titbit.

ME
>   Sorry.

I feel terrible. I've received but not given. So I decide to
make something up, something unverifiable. I mention a
powerful media banker in New York.

ME (CONT'D)
>   Know him?

MY FRIEND (V.O.)
>   Know him? Sure!

ME
>   I heard that he has cancer.

MY FRIEND (V.O.)
>   Oh, is that out?

CUT TO:
My friend will never be caught unknowing. He's heard
everything first, even if it's a lie that I just made up.

CUT TO:
INT. CITRUS RESTAURANT – DAY
I'm having lunch with my agent. I mention the gossip
about the network president.

ME

Did you hear about it?

MY AGENT

Hear about it? It was in the paper for Godsakes.

ME

It was? Where? In the business section?

MY AGENT

No! In the real estate section. There was an item in it about [my agent mentions the name of a major player in the television business who has, up until now, lived in New York] and how he and his family are moving back to LA. They bought a huge house in the Palisades which means he got a big signing bonus. That can only mean one thing. C'mon! Don't you read the paper?

The main course arrives.

MY AGENT (CONT'D)

Did you hear about [my agent mentions the name of a New York media banker]? He's dying. Of leukemia. They're giving him three months.

CUT TO:

Gossip is only truly interesting if it's about people and situations that have no direct impact on the listener. If it was our network president being replaced, it wouldn't be gossip. It would be bad news.

CUT TO:

INT. MY OFFICE – DAY

Later that week, we discover that the network president may quit, be fired, or stay, but in any case, someone is being brought in at a higher level. It is an indication of the current Hollywood mania for fancy titles that there is a position above 'Network President.'

My agent calls. I ask about the situation.

MY AGENT (V.O.)

How the hell should I know? I was just over there with another client, pitching a new series.

ME

Really? But aren't things up in the air over there? Aren't they in disarray?

MY AGENT (V.O.)

Yeah. But how is that different from every other place?

ME

Well . . .

MY AGENT (V.O.)

Look, I salute the uniform. No matter who's wearing it this week. They want to make a donkey a network president, you know what? I'll tell my clients to pitch to the donkey.

ME

I guess that makes sense.

MY AGENT (V.O.)

Now, on to other matters. Let's talk about your show. The rumor is that . . . which . . .

—st . . . and they think . . . tried to tell them
. . . you should . . . to stop . . . wh . . .

ME

I can't understand you.

MY AGENT (V.O.)

What . . . can . . . into canyon . . .

CUT TO:

I hear later that the actor who got cranked in the agency
lobby was not, in fact, cranked in the agency lobby. His
two-timing girlfriend, I hear later, was not, in fact two-
timing him, but was a committed serial monogamist. The
agent's assistant, I learn later, wasn't 6 feet tall, wasn't
buffed and cut, wasn't involved with the girl at all, except
for a desultory dinner date months ago, after which the
girl declared her non-interest and the agent's assistant
began stalking her and sending nasty letters to her
boyfriend, the actor.

The actor shows up at the agency lobby with one of
the letters and a polite request to the agent's assistant to
stop sending them. No one is beaten up. No one is promoted. The agent's assistant, though, is fired weeks later
for being 'creepy.'

I'm pretty sure this is an accurate account, but I'll keep
reading the real estate section to be sure.

CUT TO:

INT. FOUR SEASONS HOTEL ROOM, NEW
YORK CITY – MORNING

SFX: Phone rings.

ME

  (groggy, waking up)

  Hello?

MY AGENT (V.O.)

  I'm going to a Hillary Clinton fundraiser tonight!

ME

  Oh, gosh. Well. That's very nice but I'm meeting an old friend from college for dinner and—

MY AGENT (V.O.)

  I wasn't inviting you. Do you know who gave me these tickets? *Tom Hanks*. He *gave* me these tickets.

ME

  Then why are you telling me this?

MY AGENT (V.O.)

  Are you kidding? I'm telling everybody this.

ME

  But—

MY AGENT (V.O.)

  Look, the reason I called is to tell you that I haven't heard anything official yet.

ME

  What have you heard?

MY AGENT (V.O.)

  Nothing official.

ME
What have you heard that's unofficial?

MY AGENT (V.O.)
Unofficial?

ME
Unofficial.

MY AGENT (V.O.)
Nothing unofficial.

ME
What's the rumor?

MY AGENT (V.O.)
Don't talk to me about rumors. Rumors are rumors. They *swirl*. That's what they do. They *swirl* and they *fly*.

ME
But isn't the rumor always true?

MY AGENT (V.O.)
Where did you hear that? Where do you pick up this *bullshit*?

ME
Name me one time when the rumor turned out not to be true. One time.

MY AGENT (V.O.)
Okay. That's easy.

A long silence.

MY AGENT (V.O.) (CONT'D)
What, you mean *now*?

ME
Yeah.

MY AGENT (V.O.)
Can it wait until I'm back in my office? I
need to refer to my notes.

ME
See?

MY AGENT (V.O.)
Okay! Okay! The rumor is your show is dead,
okay? Are you happy? And yes, yes, it usually – okay, mostly – okay, *always* – turns
out that the rumor is true. There. You made
me say it. Satisfied?

ME
(after a pause)
But there's still a chance, right?

MY AGENT (V.O.)
Of course! Of *course*! Yes. Yes, there is still
a chance.

ME
Really?

MY AGENT (V.O.)
Yes!

ME
Really?

MY AGENT (V.O.)
Why are you doing this to me?

CUT TO:

The format of the American sitcom is so indelibly etched
into the consciousness of its audience that it's easy to

forget that the whole thing was invented in the 1950s by Desi Arnaz.

Desi – now and forever known best as 'Lucy's husband' in the long-running Ur-sitcom of the 1950s, *I Love Lucy* – came up with the money-saving system of shooting a sitcom all at once, like a stage play, while three cameras zoomed back and forth filming the action from three angles.

Desi wasn't much of an actor. *I Love Lucy* has been in continuous reruns since the 1960s, and his over-the-top reactions and finger-in-a-light-socket doubletakes don't get better with age. And when one considers that Desi Arnaz, a Cuban-American band leader married to a redhead named Lucy, was unconvincing in his portrayal of 'Ricky Ricardo,' a Cuban-American band leader married to a redhead named Lucy, well, in the words of a studio executive acquaintance describing a young male star, 'It's hard to know what he brought to the party, talent-wise.'

What Desi brought to the party, talent-wise, was something unheard of since in on-screen talent: he brought financial sophistication. He knew what a half-hour television show should cost, and he knew how to make it cost just a few dollars less. He put the cameras on wheels because it was a cheap solution to cost-prohibitive multiple takes of a scene, and because it guaranteed that a sitcom could be shot in one evening with one audience.

St Desi, the patron saint of sitcom producers, is the stuff of legend. In the old Nicodell restaurant on Melrose Avenue – now, fittingly, flattened into a parking lot –

people in the business would point to a certain booth (never the same one, but that's not important) and say, 'That's where Desi told William Frawley that if he ever showed up drunk to an *I Love Lucy* rehearsal, he wouldn't get paid for the day.' And the most famous Desi tale: when he and Lucy wanted to leave Manhattan – which was, at the time, the center of television production – for Los Angeles – which was, at the time, too far away from network headquarters for adequate supervision, the network demanded that he and Lucy agree to a pay cut, which they did, but in return, Desi asked for 100 per cent ownership of all episodes of *I Love Lucy*. The network readily agreed. After all, it reasoned, what possible value could there be in an already-broadcast episode of a sitcom?

Desi was no fool. He knew he wasn't an actor. Or a band leader. He was a businessman, or as my friend the studio executive puts it, 'a businessman in The Business.'

I am in The Business, but I'm not a businessman, and this perhaps is why I'm in New York, at the Four Seasons Hotel, waiting to hear officially that the show I have been working on for the past year is cancelled.

For some reason, the major networks announce their new schedules in New York, though they have all long-since followed Desi and Lucy to Los Angeles. Traditionally, these decisions are made in New York by Los Angeles-based executives for two reasons: one, the various media buyers and advertising executives are planted in Manhattan; and two, executives of all stripes in all industries get an erotic charge from eating a $35 room-service breakfast.

But because they've flown out here, we've flown out here. And so did all of the big agents. And the studios. And the other producers and writers who are vying for spots on the fall schedules. We're all here because . . . well, we're here ostensibly because if the network wants a last-minute creative meeting, or an adjustment or two to an existing series, we'll be available. But as far as I can fathom, we're really all here for two reasons: to get wildly, lower-lip sagging drunk, and to give money to Hillary Clinton.

The following happened a year or two ago:

A television network was thrashing out its schedule but the executives hit a snag. With only one slot to fill, and three possible choices, they simply couldn't identify the most promising candidate. The execs dithered for a day or two in their New York hotel rooms, screening and re-screening each pilot, trying to develop some kind of intuitive, gut-based sense of each show, and trying, if you'll permit the phrase, to rely on their own taste when they gave up and made a courageous decision: they ordered up another focus group. But it would have to be a fast one.

Each network unveils its fall schedule to great fanfare and huge expense, jetting in the stars of the show, laying on a buffet spread heavy on pricey shellfish, all to convince the advertising community that an upcoming show about, say, four young people interacting in a sexy fashion will be different, better, funnier, and longer-lasting than the dozens of other shows that the other networks are offering about, say, four young people interacting in a sexually-charged but basically chaste arena.

But to do that you need to decide *which* show you're going to schedule so you can know *which* actors and actresses to jet into Manhattan for glad-handing and ass-kissing the advertisers.

You see the dilemma: the network under discussion hadn't made its final decision with the press conference only twelve hours away. The solution? Fly the casts of ALL *three* programs to New York on the *same* plane. In the intervening six hours, collect the results of the last-minute focus group and make the decision. When the plane lands, gather the casts in the airport lounge, whisk some of them into Manhattan and into stardom; tell the others to slink home.

This solution contains all you need to know about Hollywood. It has it all: extravagance, procrastination, cruelty masquerading as efficiency, and focus groups.

CUT TO:
INT. REGENCY HOTEL BAR – MANHATTAN
– NIGHT
I am sitting at the bar waiting to meet a friend. I know personally, or have worked with, or know people who have worked with, every single person in the bar. An agent slaps me on the back. His eyes are red and his tie is askew.

    AGENT
     Hey man.

ME

  Hi.

AGENT

  Let me buy you a drink.

ME

  Thanks, but I'm on my way out.

AGENT

  Then let me give you two tickets to the Hillary
  Clinton thing.

ME

  Gee, that's very generous of you.

AGENT

  Look, from me to you, let me just say, I'm
  sorry about your show man.

ME

  Why do you say that? What have you heard?

AGENT

  Ooops. Hey man if you don't know then I
  don't know, okay?

I look down at my drink. The agent looks around, guiltily.

AGENT (CONT'D)

  I feel terrible that you heard it from me, man.

  I mean, not that you heard it from me, but

  that you heard it from me when I'm so . . .

The agent begins staring at an attractive young woman
who has just entered the bar.

ME

  So . . . wasted?

The agent moves off.

32

> AGENT
> (to attractive woman) Would you like to meet
> Hillary Clinton?

CUT TO:
A few years back, a well-known comic actor hosted his own late-night talk show. The show received dismal ratings, terrible reviews, and midway through its thirteen-week run, it was cancelled.

So it was odd, only a few days after such a spectacular and public failure, to see the actor sitting at an outside table at the old Columbia Bar & Grill – now something called *Pinot Hollywood & Martini Bar* – having lunch with a couple of friends. Odd because in his shoes I'd be thousands of miles away for months; and odd because he didn't look that great. He didn't look tanned or rested; hadn't had a quick eye tuck or chin implant; didn't laugh loudly or smile nonchalantly. He looked, instead, like a guy who just got his ass handed to him on national television.

It was a heroic performance – the bravest lunch I've yet seen eaten. And as he ate and chatted with his party, Industry types would pat him on the back or give him a 'thumbs-up' gesture as they passed. A few would murmur 'Good for you;' some would claim, loudly, 'I loved the show;' and some really smart ones would opt for the sophisticated surgical strike compliment: 'My *kids* really *were wild* about that show.'

In much the same way that the audience at an Oscar

ceremony a few years ago gave Christopher Reeve a tearful, hand-reddening ovation – not for *Superman III* or *The Bostonians* but for, let's face it, falling off a horse – the lunchtime crowd at the old Columbia Bar & Grill wanted this actor to know that *they* knew how tough it was for him to eat lunch out on the sunny patio, and that they applauded his bravery and wished him the best. It's often said about people in this business, mostly by people *not* in this business, that we're heartless and unforgiving. Not true. We relish failure. We wallow in misfortune. We live to applaud the down-and-out.

So it was not surprising to see the parade of well-wishers file by that afternoon. One of them, a guy in the international television distribution arm of a large studio – a guy I *knew* didn't know the actor from a hole in the ground – walked by him, stopped, put his hands on the guy's shoulders, leaned down, and *kissed the failed talk-show host on the top of the head*. And while I could not bring myself to go that far, the spirit of full disclosure requires me to admit that, when our eyes briefly met across the restaurant patio as happens occasionally in public places (I wasn't staring at the man, honest) I caught myself giving him, a man I haven't met either, a raised-eyebrow-rueful-smile greeting.

CUT TO:
INT. HOTEL ELEVATOR – NIGHT
An executive from another network steps into the elevator after me.

34

EXECUTIVE
> Hi!

ME
> Hi.

EXECUTIVE
> I'm off to see Hillary.

ME
> Great.

EXECUTIVE
> What are you in town for?

ME
> Well ... you see ... our show is ... we
> thought there might be a chance ...

I trail off.

ME (CONT'D)
> To visit a sick relative.

CUT TO:

Because the thrill of raiding the minibar and ordering room service and gratuitously dry-cleaning my clothes at the studio's expense has worn off, I bite the bullet and actually go to the Hillary Clinton fundraiser. My enjoyment of the event is marred somewhat by two things: one, I'm not a Hillary Clinton supporter; and two, right before she starts to speak, an executive from our network approaches me with a sad, wan smile on her face, and whispers 'You're not on the fall schedule' in my ear, and then, as the senator begins her speech, the executive adds, 'probably,' and moves off.

I do not do the Desi-thing. The Desi-thing to do would

be to head back to the hotel, catch the next plane home to Los Angeles, and start planning the next show. Instead, I head back to the hotel, get drunk, and send my pyjamas out to be dry-cleaned and pressed.

I don't have the Desi in me. I'll never be a businessman in The Business.

CUT TO:
INT. FOUR SEASONS HOTEL NEW YORK –
DAY
I'm in my room. It's four in the afternoon. I stare at the phone. It rings.

 ME
  Hello?
 MY AGENT (V.O.)
  Still moping? Go out! Carouse!
 ME
  What do you want?
 MY AGENT (V.O.)
  I want to tell you that your show was offi-
  cially cancelled fifteen minutes ago. I'm trying
  to use my sad voice, but it's hard, because
  I've got two other clients who got their shows
  ordered, and I've been using my happy voice
  most of the day, so forgive me.
 ME
  Thanks.
 MY AGENT (V.O.)
  Remember that you did a bunch of hilarious

and excellent episodes of television, and for what it's worth, the conversations I've had with everyone are all about you and your partner and how great you are. In fact, the president of another network stopped me in the Bergdorf Goodman elevator to tell me that he would, in his words, 'pay anything' to get your next show for his network.

ME

He said that? Really?

MY AGENT (V.O.)

Really.

ME

Wow.

MY AGENT (V.O.)

As long as it's a male-driven comedy, because those are the only ones that make any money in reruns.

ME

I see.

MY AGENT (V.O.)

So get going! Start writing!

ME

I don't know. I don't know if I have another one in me.

MY AGENT (V.O.)

What? What are you talking about?

ME

I'm just saying I feel like I'm stuck in a bad

pattern – we do a show, they put it on, they take it off, we do a show, they put it on, they take it off. It's like we're in this awful rhythm – do a show, get cancelled, do a show, get cancelled, like, like . . .

MY AGENT (V.O.)

Some kind of sitcom script?

ME

Yeah.

MY AGENT (V.O.)

What's wrong with that?

A long pause.

ME

I don't know what's wrong with that, actually.

MY AGENT (V.O.)

I mean, it works for half-hour comedy.

ME

Yeah, but I'm not sure life really follows the patterns of situation comedy structure.

MY AGENT (V.O.)

You aren't?

ME

You *are*?

MY AGENT (V.O.)

I have a teenager at home and an elderly parent in the early stages of Alzheimer's. Trust me. It does. It really really *really* does.

CUT TO:

Charlie Chaplin once explained that there are two ways to film the old guy-slips-on-a-banana-peel joke. The first, unfunny, way goes like this: cut to the guy walking, oblivious. Cut to the banana peel, lying in wait. Cut to a wide shot of the guy approaching the banana peel. Cut to a close-up of the banana peel, just as the guy's foot hits it. Cut back to the wide shot, as the guy slips on the peel and lands on his rear end, which as everyone knows from cartoons, is the funniest part of the human body and one which registers no real pain.

The second, funny, way to film that same sequence is as follows: cut to the guy, walking. Cut to the banana peel, lying in wait. Cut to a wide shot of the guy approaching the banana peel. Cut to a close-up of the banana peel, just as the guy's foot *almost* hits it. Cut back to the wide shot, as the guy deftly steps over the banana peel, smiling smugly . . . and falls into an open manhole.

Get the difference? The trick is to make sure the audience never knows which part is the set up and which part is the joke. Until they start laughing.

When I got back home, a friend of mine told me the story about the network and the three casts. After I finished commiserating bitterly, which in Hollywood means explaining how the situation is much *much* worse in my case, she told me the quaint finish.

Apparently, in the confusion, one of the actors from one of the castoff programs got mixed in with the chosen ones, and was whisked into Manhattan, where he dutifully attended the press conference, charmed the advertisers, gorged himself on grilled lobster, and ran up $13,000 worth of hotel charges, most of which, it was hinted at darkly, were for hotel-supplied hookers.

That's a guy who takes bad news gracefully.

FADE OUT.

A phone call, Friday, 4:30 PM

'Hi!'
  'Hi.'
  'I just wanted to say how much fun it was working
with you.'
  'Um . . . thanks.'
  'I just . . . it's just such a pleasure to work with a writer
who really feels passionate about his project.'
  'Well, thanks, Trish.'
  'Tori.'
  'Tori.'
  'And I wanted to say that I'll miss you.'
  'Oh. Well, I'm sorry to hear that. I guess my next ques-
tion is, which one of us is leaving?'
  'Hahahahahaha.'
  'No, seriously. Which one of us?'
  'Me! Didn't you see it in the trades? I'm going to another
opportunity.'
  'Oh. Well congratulations.'

'Thanks. Please hold for Josh.'

'Hi!'

'Hi, Josh.'

'Hey there!'

'Hi, it's Josh, too.'

'Hi.'

'I'm in the car with Josh and you're on speaker.'

'And we're here in the office, me and Tori and Jamal and Eli, on conference.'

'Okay.'

'We read the pages.'

'Oh, okay. I just sent them along so you could get a flavor of . . .'

'You know, I always want to start out positive and keep things real collegial, okay?'

'Okay.'

'So on the positive side, we're no longer concerned that this thing may not be long enough.'

'Oh.'

'But we're a little concerned that it's just all about failure.'

'So far.'

'Right. Thanks, Eli. So far in the pages that you've given us.'

'And about how bad you feel getting another show cancelled and how many failures and setbacks you've experienced.'

'I don't think it's "many" failures, really. I've been pretty successful, I think.'

'The first thirty pages aren't very up, is what we're saying.'

'Oh. Right. See, what I was going for was . . .'

'It's just that we don't have a lot of success with projects about aging failures scrambling for money.'

'Aging failures?'

'I'm just responding to the pages.'

'We really want everyone who comes into contact with the project to like you.'

'I do, too.'

'Great!'

'Great!'

'Great!'

'So maybe I should make some adjustments in those pages and sort of lighten the tone, make me – I mean, the narrator guy – more likable.'

'I think it would really help it out a lot.'

'Let me work on that.'

'Great!'

'Great!'

'Great meeting!'

'Great meeting!'

SUMMER: 'IS THERE A SHOW IN THAT?'

FADE IN:

Hollywood has two pompous nicknames for itself: 'The Business' and 'The Industry.' Both names pack an ironic punch: calling it 'The Business' must surely elicit a sickly smile from shareholders of the Sony, Vivendi, and AOL/Time Warner Corporations, who are probably still waiting for the spending to stop and the business to begin; while the nickname 'The Industry' – with its connotation of industriousness – is equally silly when one considers that the most prevalent activity on any soundstage or location shoot is the reading of magazines and the eating of pastries.

Still, the beehive that is Hollywood manages to churn out enough news, gossip, and press releases to fill two daily newspapers, *Variety* and its scrappier cousin, the *Hollywood Reporter*. Around here, we call them the 'trades' – short for 'trade papers' – and they are read with bitter intensity every morning by anyone who's anyone, and anyone who's *trying* to be anyone, in The Business.

Walk through the various breakfast spots in Los Angeles, and it's easy to spot the out-of-towners. They're the ones reading the trades in public. Out-of-towners think that *Variety* and the *Reporter* are filled with interesting Industry news – stock quotes, reviews, box-office figures, that kind of thing – and, of course, they are. But the more practiced reader, the Industry denizen, reads the trades for one reason and one reason only: to find out how much other people are being paid. And as this leads almost inevitably to violently obscene language, reading the trades is something to be done in private.

CUT TO:
EXT. STUDIO PARKING LOT – DAY
I walk to my office.

My writing partner and I have recovered, slightly, from our recent cancellation and we are now back at work, trying to come up with another series. In Hollywood, failure is like childbirth – it's messy and painful and often requires hospitalization, but when it's all over, some magic amnesia takes place and you can't wait to do it again.

This isn't really an act of heroic non-sulking. It's our job, actually. We have what is called an 'Overall Deal' at a large studio. Which means, essentially, that they pay us a tidy sum to come up with, write, produce, cast, and generally generate television shows, which we then try to sell to the various television networks.

It's a great system, but it doesn't make much economic sense. In baseball parlance, we're being paid to 'swing for the fence,' to aim for a monster hit. Because one monster hit generates enough profit for the studio to pay for everyone else's failures. At least, that's how the system is supposed to work.

CUT TO:
INT. MY OFFICE – CONTINUOUS
My assistant tosses *Variety* at me with a sadistic glee.
MY ASSISTANT
   Page three.
ME
   Good morning.
MY ASSISTANT
   It won't be when you read page three.

CUT TO:
INSERT SHOT: PAGE THREE OF *VARIETY*
An article reports that a television writer – a friend of mine – has recently signed a deal with a studio for a whopping huge sum.

CUT TO:
CLOSE-UP: ME, READING
I am aware that my eyes are bulging out of their sockets. I am aware that my face is getting red. I am aware that the entire office staff – a staff, I'm sure, convinced that I'm an overpaid, under-worked complainer (a charac-

terization that I do not dispute) – is watching me intensely.

I muster a smile.

ME
(croaky voice)
Good for him! I'm happy for him. Really.

CUT TO:
Later, alone, in my office, I attack a pocket calculator with violent stabs of my finger. I am making a desperate and pathetic attempt to crunch the numbers in his deal and crunch the numbers in my deal and still come out ahead. I do this for several minutes. Huge rolls of calculator tape spill out over my desk.

It is only when I've run the calculator's batteries down that I stop this childish and deeply unattractive behavior. I should know better. I've been in this business long enough to have learned this immutable law: no matter how much money you make, someone is always making slightly more. It is hardwired into the circuitry of The Industry, and it is what makes things here hum with the ruthless efficiency that pure uncut greed produces.

The office upstairs is occupied by a television writer who also has a big contract at the studio. As I sit in my chair, heart rate returning to normal, angry facial rictus relaxing, eyes slowly changing from envy-green to normal-blue, I can hear the guy upstairs come into his office. I can hear him greet his assistant. I can hear him take a seat behind his desk. I can hear the rustle of *Variety*. And

I'm pretty sure, if I tilt my head just right, I can make out the clickety-clack of his calculator as it works and worries the numbers.

CUT TO:
INT. MY OFFICE – DAY
The phone rings.

> MY AGENT (V.O.)
>> How's the development coming? Any hot ideas?

> ME
>> Hard to say.

> MY AGENT (V.O.)
>> Hard to say? C'mon. Perk up here. This is show business. I want you to have fun.

> ME
>> What?

> MY AGENT (V.O.)
>> And you should want you to have fun.

> ME
>> Well, to tell you the truth—

> MY AGENT (V.O.)
>> I don't want to hear this. This is about the deal in the trades, right?

> ME
>> Well, as a matter of fact—

> MY AGENT (V.O.)
>> I don't want to hear this. But I'm right, right? Tell me I'm right.

ME

You're right. It seems that every day I read in the trades about someone else's big money deal at some other studio to do exactly the same job as I'm doing – no, a worse job, actually, because we get shows on the air, and these guys haven't done that – and I can't help but think that I'm a chump and you're too complacent.

MY AGENT (V.O.)

So when I say 'I don't want to hear this,' you hear what, exactly? 'Please tell me all about it?' I'm interested in the way your mind works.

ME

You know what? This isn't a fruitful conversation.

MY AGENT (V.O.)

Can I tell you something that I hope makes you feel better? The trades only report a fraction of the deals around town that are better than yours. There are more deals better than yours in town than there are stars in the heavens.

ME

Umm . . .

MY AGENT (V.O.)

Don't interrupt. This wind-up has a big finish, I promise you. But those deals are just *temporary*, you see. They won't last. Those guys

will make a nice pot of change for a year or
two—

ME

Or three. Or five.

MY AGENT (V.O.)

Let me *finish*. I'm telling you, it's worth it.
Anyway, you guys have a great track record.
You get shows on the air. And you'll get
another one on the air very *very* soon.

A pause.

MY AGENT (V.O.)

Right?

ME

Right.

MY AGENT (V.O.)

Let me *finish*. Anyway, the point is, you're
building equity in a big, big payoff – that *I*
negotiated, *okay?* – after only three or four
years of your series, a payoff, may I just add,
that will make all of those development deals
seem pathetic and hopelessly threadbare. You
can thank me now if you're feeling gracious.

ME

Really?

MY AGENT (V.O.)

Really. Keep your eye on the brass ring, kid.
Don't get distracted by gold fever.

ME

But what if our show gets cancelled again?

What if we never make it to year three or
four?

MY AGENT (V.O.)

Well, then you were right the first time.

ME

Excuse me?

MY AGENT (V.O.)

Then you *are* a chump.

ME

Interesting point. But what about a new studio
deal?

MY AGENT (V.O.)

What about it?

ME

Well, we've got a year left on the current one.
What I'm asking is, if we don't get another
show on the air this year, do you think the
studio will offer us another contract?

MY AGENT (V.O.)

What do you want me to say? That somehow
the huge, industry-wide cost-cutting purge is
going to sort of swerve around you? Make a
you-specific exception?

ME

I'd like that.

MY AGENT (V.O.)

Did you spend all the money?

ME

No.

MY AGENT (V.O.)
Really?
ME
Really.
MY AGENT (V.O.)
Really?
ME
Really.
MY AGENT (V.O.)
Look, do you want me to be honest? Really honest?
ME
I don't know. Do I?
MY AGENT (V.O.)
Probably not. But I'm going to be anyway. The business has changed, okay? Radically, radically changed. There are no big studio deals out there anymore. The era of big deals is over.
ME
Then what about that deal in the trades? That guy's agent got him a lot of money.
MY AGENT (V.O.)
What is this? Dump on me day? Look, that deal in the trades? The one you've got such *tsuris* about? That's pretty much the last deal you'll be reading about for a while. The town is broke, okay? It's not a deal. It's a *death rattle*.

ME

So you're saying that when our deal is up the studio won't want to re-up us?

MY AGENT (V.O.)

I'm saying deals are over. And you've got exactly one year left on yours. So do you want to spend what could easily be your last year making guaranteed serious money moping and whining and making vicious personal attacks on me, or getting another show on the air?

ME

So you're saying that it's unlikely that there's a deal after this deal?

MY AGENT (V.O.)

I quibble with the term 'unlikely.'

ME

So you're saying—

MY AGENT (V.O.)

You keep saying 'So you're saying' like you're listening to what I'm saying, but you're obviously having a hard time with this. This is some kind of personality disorder thing. I'm telling you, okay, I'm telling you that you have one year left, okay, on a deal that no one is ever going to get again, okay? That's what I'm saying. I'm saying it, I said it, I'm done.

ME

You're telling me this *now*?

MY AGENT (V.O.)

Oh come on. What did you want me to do? Call you up a few months ago and say, 'Let me tell you what I'm hearing out in the marketplace. I'm hearing money is tight. I'm hearing that somewhere between TiVo and Osama bin Laden and fifty bazillion cable channels, things got squeezed pretty thin? That there's no more big money in television? That there are no more big-money studio deals? Make sure you save your money because in the not-too-distant future we're all going to be looking back on these days and thinking to ourselves, *Wow! We all lived through a truly historic era when writers were paid huge sums of money and now that era's over and it will never ever ever ever repeat itself.* Is that what you have in mind?

ME

Would have been nice.

MY AGENT

I agree. But I hadn't put it all together until just now.

SFX: Click. Dial tone.

CUT TO:

In this business, timing is your most important friend. And in the television business, in which each issue of the *Wall Street Journal* seems to signal a new direction, the perfect time to sign a deal was anytime directly before, or directly after, we signed ours. And the *Journal* agrees with my agent on another important detail: the money wheel has stopped spinning. No more fat writers' contracts.

But I'm grateful to be working. A year left to go on a studio contract is a lot better than no contract at all.

I had lunch with an old friend of mine, a guy who has spent a Hollywood lifetime (that's roughly fifteen years) working in the television business. He hasn't had an easy time of it recently. He hasn't worked in two years.

I do know a lot of writers who are currently either not working, or working for a lot less than they used to. I'm sure some blame it on the recent popularity of reality shows, but I tend to blame it on the huge glut of sitcoms that were on in the late 1990s, leading to huge development deals and inflated salaries, leading to, inevitably, a market correction. Leading to no more development deals.

The people in trouble are the ones who made the same mistake overpaid people have always made, in all businesses: they spent the money. Or, worse, they *got used* to the money.

So last week, when my friend called me for lunch, I knew who was buying.

We pulled up in our respective cars at the same time, and as he was getting out of his, he smiled weakly.

'What do you think?' he asked, jerking his thumb at the car.

'Nice,' I said. It was a Chevrolet station wagon. The guy has kids. What was I supposed to say?

'Yeah, well,' he mumbles, 'I had to cut back. Dump the Lexus.'

'Still, that's a nice car,' I said.

'It's a *shitty* car,' he said bitterly. 'I have to tell everyone that it's my *wife's* car. And still they treat me like dirt.'

He turns to the valet parking attendant. 'Be careful with my wife's car, okay, *amigo*?' Then he turned and peered into the restaurant. 'Do you think they saw me drive up? If they did, sorry, man. We'll get a rotten table.'

'C'mon,' I said. 'People don't care about stuff like that. That's just an LA myth.'

He looked at me and shook his head sourly. Then he brightened. 'But they saw *you* drive up too. And your car is *nice*.'

The truth is, I have two cars – a silly Los Angeles extravagance, I know, but in my defense, one of them is a real shit pile. It runs intermittently, makes peculiar noises, and at speeds under 50 miles-per-hour emits an odor that smells like neither gasoline nor oil, but, instead, like burning human flesh. But I love that car, and can't get rid of it for some strange sentimental reason, so when I bought my German sleek-mobile, I kept the shit pile in the garage alongside it. I like to think that the two cars, after some initial sniping, have reached an understanding, sitting there quietly, side-by-side in the dark. Perhaps the shit pile keeps the German sleek-mobile honest and humble, in an all-flesh-is-grass sort of way. And the German car, in return, reminds the shit pile that he is, in fact, a shit pile, and too many won't-starts and sickly-smells and it's out the door.

A few days after that, I had lunch at a place that my writing partner and I go to at least once a week. It's a standard Italian restaurant (bad bread, illegible menu, obscure Italian fizzy water) but it's been a serviceable feeding place for years.

The valet guy looked at my car.

'Everything okay, chief?' he asked, in a tone of voice that, even through his thick Chiapas accent was clearly pitying.

'Yeah, fine,' I said, not quite getting it.

'Where's the other car?' he asked. 'The nice one?'

'Home,' I said, my voice strangely high-pitched. I mean, it *was* home. In the garage. But for some reason I decided to drive the other one to work, something I'd never done. I think of it as a weekend car, a drive-the-dog-to-the-beach car.

'So everything's goin' okay then, chief?' he asked again, with a face out of a Latin romantic tragedy.

'Yes,' I said, too indignant to be convincing. I pulled out of the restaurant. In the rearview mirror, I could see his face, his pitying, sad-eyed, poor-*gringo* face, peering at me.

And driving back to the studio, I realize that I'd been experiencing that scene, in varying tempos, all day. The pretty girl at Peet's Coffee that morning saw me drive up for the first time, and for the first time she was, like, diffident. People on the freeway wouldn't let me pass. At the time, I attributed it to heavy traffic, or a lurking highway cop, but the truth, as I now realize, is that people in Los Angeles *do not get out of the way for crappy cars.* It's Lexus or better around here.

And the guard at the studio gate – a gate I've been driving through with a cheery wave for *twelve* years – that day he gave me the fish-eye, the not-so-fast-fella, the you're-bringing-that-bag-of-bones-in-*here*? look.

The next morning, dashing off to work, I reached for my car keys. My hand stopped, suspended over the two different sets. I thought to myself: Am I going to play the silly money-obsessed game? Or am I going to thumb my nose at the foolishness of the Hollywood machine? Am I going to surrender to a tawdry set of values, to a sick craving for status and misbegotten respect? Or am I going to forge my own set of standards? Am I, finally, a man or a mouse? Who am I? (Or, at least, who am I *today*?) I'm not going to tell you which set of keys I took. I don't want you to think less of me. Or more of me. Depending, I guess, on you.

CUT TO:
INT. 'THE RODEO ROOM' BEVERLY REGENT
HOTEL – DAY
I am at a large lunch for a United States senator. He is speaking about the 'sacred trust' that Americans place in what he calls 'the media professionals.' I am staring down at my sorrel soup, trying to avoid the gaze of his chief fundraiser, who is sitting opposite.

An agent I know is sitting next to me. He puts his hand on my shoulder and gives it a squeeze. I have been in

Hollywood long enough to know that he will next slip his hand up to my neck and lean in to whisper into my ear. This is weird the first couple of times, and then, suddenly, it isn't weird anymore.

> AGENT
> (whispering)
> So, what, you've got an overall deal somewhere?

I nod.

> AGENT (CONT'D)
> When did you sign?

> ME
> Two years ago.

His face squinches up in agony.

> AGENT
> Oooo.

> ME
> Yeah, well.

> AGENT
> So you got the up tick but not the bonanza
> and it's killing you.

> ME
> Well, it's not *killing* me.

> AGENT
> I tell all my clients, 'Bank the dough because
> this will *never happen again.*'

> ME
> (mumbling)
> It's not *killing* me.

He squeezes my neck.

SET UP. JOKE. SET UP. JOKE

ME
(mumbling)
I've got my health. I'm young.

The agent puts his finger to his lips.

AGENT
Shhh. I'm trying to hear the senator.

CUT TO:

I got the up tick but not the bonanza, which I hope will never be a suitable title for my autobiography.

The only sure way to reap the bonanza, unfortunately, is to come up with a great idea. Which is hard work. Who knows where ideas come from?

A screenwriter I know once wrote a script about a screenwriter who cheats on his wife. In the script, the screenwriter's wife is fat, shrewish, and is hit by a bus on page 97.

In real life, the screenwriter's wife is nice-looking, pleasant, and because she lives in Los Angeles, hasn't been *near* a bus in fifteen years. Still, she was deeply upset by her husband's script.

'Is that supposed to be me?' she wanted to know.

'No, no,' he assured her.

'Then who is it?' she demanded tearfully.

'It's my first wife,' he said.

'And who's this slut bitch your character meets at a Starbucks and fucks in the backseat of the Lexus?' she wailed.

'That's you,' he answered. Then added, helpfully, 'Don't you remember how we got together?'

She still wanted to know about the bus accident. In real life, his first wife was alive and well and collecting eleven thousand court-ordered dollars every month from him. So what's the deal, she wanted to know, with the bus thing?

'That, darling,' he said, 'is where I did some writing.'

A friend of mine told me the following story, which I assume is true because it doesn't involve money:

He and his partner had just worked out a treatment for a new animated series. Armed with drawings and sample dialogue, full-color renditions of all of the characters, and even some sample voices, they march to the office of the studio president to present their show.

The new series follows the life of a perpetual loser – a panicky guy who's a cog-in-the-wheel, lives with his parents, brims with unrequited lust, surfs the internet for free pornography, you know the type – and chronicles his triumphs (few) and his humiliations (many). Think Charlie Brown all grown up and you'll have the idea.

In an act of inadvertent cruelty, though, they based many attributes of their lead character – including, unbelievably, his appearance – on one of the presidents of the studio. Sometimes the creative process is like that: you can spend months and months recreating what you already know, and bits of your familiar life appear, even in something as trivial as a treatment, as out-of-the-blue-sky wholesale fantasy. It never occurred to them that they had modeled a character after this guy until they were in his office with a few other executives getting 'notes' on the treatment.

'Getting notes' is a little like 'writing a treatment,' only in reverse. It's the lazy executive's tool: it allows him to do what he does best and likes to do (talk), while freeing him from doing what he does poorly and doesn't enjoy (make sense). The writer's responsibility is to nod, jot down a few illegible notes, and pipe up, every now and then, with a cheerful 'you may be right' and a thoughtful 'we'll take a look at that.'

Halfway through the notes, the executive picks up the sketch of the main character – a sketch, essentially, of a younger him – and taps it thoughtfully. As he looks at the sketch and chews his lower lip, my friend's eyes dart back and forth between the two of them, and suddenly, like an ice cube down his back, he sees what he has done. His partner makes a similar realization and freezes, pen poised over pad.

'It seems a little familiar,' the executive says, slowly, and they know that they're sunk. He's insulted, hurt, furious – he'll take this whole episode as an elaborate insult delivered in his office and with his money. They'll have poisoned the friendly relationship they have with him and the studio – a relationship that allowed them a huge amount of autonomy – and nine months from now they'll be assigned to a crappy show they broadcast in the afternoons, aimed at kids with no friends.

'Familiar?' my friend asks. If it's possible for a voice to sweat, his was sweating. 'How so?' he continued. 'Do you mean "familiar" like as in "family?" As in "this guy looks like a part of our television *family*?" Or do you mean it like "I've seen this guy somewhere before?" Because, I mean, how could you? *How could you?* It's totally made up. Like from . . .' He snaps his fingers. 'Like from thin air,' he says.

The studio chief looked at him strangely. 'No,' he says, 'I mean that the colors that the artist used look a little *Simpsons*-y. Maybe we should go more neutral.'

'We'll take a look at that,' my friend says thoughtfully.

The meeting breaks up. The junior executives file out of the office and they pack up their notes. As they leave, the executive calls them back.

'I know what you're doing,' he says, breaking into a wide grin. 'And it's hilarious.'

The sweaty voice again.

'What?' my friend asks. 'What are we doing?'

The studio chief mentions one of the junior executives who was in the meeting. 'You're basing your character on him, right?'

My friend reiterates that it's all make-believe pretend.

'You writers!' the studio president says. 'You're so mean. Funny but mean.'

And they slip out of the office.

People rarely recognize themselves. I suppose this is why so many parents of writers are still on speaking terms with their children.

CUT TO:

INT. OFFICE – DAY

We are sitting around trying to come up with a new show. Our task, for the next ten months, is to get a big idea for a series, flesh it out, write a first, or 'pilot' episode, get a network to agree to film the pilot, then get the same network to agree to make twenty-two more just like it. Simple, really.

But for now, what we really need is an idea.

What we do, essentially, is sit in our office and stare out the window in silence. Each one of us silently hopes that the other will either throw out a brilliant idea for a show, or better still, begin an off-topic conversation. Then, we can chat aimlessly for a little bit, until the one who started the off-topic conversation says something like 'I bought a new shirt this weekend,' or 'There's a new Italian restaurant in Santa Monica,' or 'I'm getting another cup of coffee,' at which point the one who *didn't* start the off-topic conversation can say, bitterly, 'Is there a show in *that*?'

SFX: Phone rings.

MY AGENT (V.O.)

Hi hi.

ME

Hi.

MY AGENT (V.O.)

So? Anything?

ME

What do you mean?

MY AGENT (V.O.)
It's been two months! What's next?

ME
We're thinking. We're noodling.

MY AGENT (V.O.)
Bullshit. You're staring out the window brooding silently and wondering why everyone else has a show on the air and you don't.

ME
What makes you think that?

MY AGENT (V.O.)
Number A, because all writers are alike, and two, because I'm standing outside your office looking in the window.

ME
What are you doing on the lot? Did you come to take us to lunch?

MY AGENT (V.O.)
No, I'm taking another client to lunch. I'd stop in and say 'hi' but I'm in a hurry. My other client has a show on the air so he's really busy.

ME
Just so you know, we're not brooding any-more.

MY AGENT (V.O.)
Good.

ME
We're just trying to come up with some-

thing that people will respond to. It's not easy.

MY AGENT (V.O.)

(soothing voice)

I know, honey. I know.

ME

So we're just taking it slow.

MY AGENT (V.O.)

Not too slow! You've only got a year.

ME

We're trying to figure out what people want.

MY AGENT (V.O.)

Oh God. Whatever you do, *don't do that*.

ME

Why?

MY AGENT (V.O.)

Just do a show that *you* want to watch. Just do a show that *you* think is interesting. That's hard enough.

ME

I'm not sure my tastes match most of America's.

MY AGENT (VO)

Want to hear something sad? I'm sure that they do.

ME

Really?

MY AGENT (V.O.)

Oh *please*. I'm so sick of people out here thinking they're so different.

ME
> What?

MY AGENT (V.O.)
> People are the same all over. You think you're the only one in America staring out the window thinking to himself, 'I hate my job?'

ME
> Oh.

MY AGENT (VO)
> Is there a show in *that*?

CUT TO:

An actor friend of mine tells the following story: he was working as a lunch-shift bartender at a swank Beverly Hills restaurant. The customers were all talking about a terrible plane crash that had occurred earlier that morning. A well-known agent stopped by the bar while waiting for his lunch guest to arrive. He overheard two customers talking about the crash. It was the first he had heard of it. 'How many people died?' he asked. They told him that the death count was somewhere between three and four hundred. He winced.

'Oh, man, how awful,' he said. 'So was there anybody on the plane?'

He didn't mean *anyone* anyone. He meant *anyone show business* anyone. He meant *anyone I have pretended to be best friends with in the past* anyone.

People who are not in show business – or, to be more specific, people who do not live in the 310 or 212 telephone area codes – are an impenetrable mystery to those of us who do. What movies they watch and why, what television shows they choose and why, what they eat, why they eat it, when they work, what they drive, and especially how on earth they seem to make do on such skimpy salaries – these thoughts obsess our waking hours. Figure them out and the world is yours. That's the chief irony of this most ironic business: only those with the common touch can afford to live like kings. Steven Spielberg is so tuned in to the sensibilities of ordinary Americans that he no longer needs to be around them. Ever.

But the truth is, America isn't all that remote from, say, Brentwood, as much as it pains Brentwood to admit it.

Once, years ago, a successful and well-respected television writer was asked by the *Los Angeles Times* to list her favorite television programs. They wanted to know, for some unfathomable reason, what someone who creates television likes to watch. She professed, like so many university professors, not to watch anything. 'You see,' she said, 'I *hate* television. Really. My husband and I *never* watch the damn thing. We don't even have cable.'

The interviewer pressed on. Surely she must watch something – the news, maybe, or the financial channel? Finally, she admitted to watching only two channels, CNN and the Discovery Channel, both of which are available exclusively on cable, which she professed not to have. Ultimately, she admitted to having cable in 'the upstairs television,' but not the 'downstairs television,' or the 'kitchen television.' By my count, that made three televisions in her house, all presumably hated and unwatched. Television has this effect on people. There it is against the wall, as big as your head, and yet no smart person ever seems to watch it. Perhaps because it conjures up a life of lonely idleness, secret snacking, and social isolation, people just don't want to admit to their TV habit. It's like masturbation for the eyes. It's not a pastime you want to advertise.

Rotten television is another matter. The same dinner companion who denies watching anything on the box will, without taking a breath, gleefully recount the latest episode of *The Littlest Groom* or *Temptation Island* or one of those talk shows where loathsome guests spew vile anger, and occasional blows, at each other. Ironic distance, I guess, makes the heart grow fonder.

Of course, I never watch the damn thing either, and certainly never waste my time with anything as awful as *Temptation Island*. This has less to do with my elevated sensibilities than my all-consuming jealousy. Why turn on the tube – even just to flip around the dial – and run the risk of seeing a show more successful and popular than any show my partner and I have ever written? Or, worse, *better* than any show my partner and I have ever written?

CUT TO:
INT. WASHINGTON, DC HOTEL BALLROOM
– NIGHT
I am at a big Washington journalists dinner. I'm the guest

of an actual White House correspondent, and until I walked into the dinner and saw 2,500 people milling around, I was thrilled and honored to get the invitation. Now, as I make my way to my table (off to the side, behind a pillar), I wonder who must have cancelled at the last minute and bequeathed my invitation.

My table is almost filled, and for a moment I'm cheered by the presence of an actual cabinet secretary two seats to my left, and not just any old cabinet secretary, but one who is currently under investigation for influence peddling. I am clearly at an important table. But my spirit quickly falls when I realize that I'm the only non-journalist at the table (I figure this out by noticing that I'm the only one – besides the cabinet secretary – who is not wearing a pre-tied bow tie) and in a few moments I'm going to be asked what I do for a living (a standard and blunt question in this bluntest of towns) and I'm going to say, 'I'm a television writer,' and everyone at the table is going to shrug and say, in staggered turns, 'Oh, I *never* watch television,' and 'I just *can't bring myself* to watch it.'

CABINET SECRETARY

What do you do?

ME

I'm a television writer.

Nods. Shrugs.

CABINET SECRETARY

Any show in particular?

I mention a few I've worked on.

WOMAN TO MY RIGHT

Oh, I *never* watch television.

MAN TO MY LEFT

I just *can't bring myself* to watch it.

MAN TO MY SECOND RIGHT

Who has the time to watch the damn thing?

CABINET SECRETARY

(pointing to me)

Hey, I liked that show.

I decide to give generously to the cabinet secretary's defense fund.

WOMAN TO MY RIGHT

I saw a cute *Raymond* last night.

MAN TO MY LEFT

Anyone know who was voted off *Survivor*?

DISSOLVE TO:

INT. WASHINGTON, DC HOTEL BALLROOM

– LATER THAT NIGHT

I'm chatting with the cabinet secretary, telling him about the various Screen Actors Guild minimums, explaining the concept of residuals, and the stylistic differences between film and videotape – he asked, by the way.

CABINET SECRETARY

So, what's the deal with syndication profit sharing? Explain that to me.

ME

Well, that's where all the real money is, actually. The studio basically pays for a show and rents it to a network. The fee the network pays, called a 'license fee,' isn't really enough to cover the cost of the show.

CABINET SECRETARY

Wait, so the studio loses money?

ME

Yeah. Until the show has enough episodes produced to syndicate—

CABINET SECRETARY

Sell into reruns?

ME

Right.

CABINET SECRETARY

Interesting. So why don't the networks just make their own shows and keep them on and keep the profits?

ME

Well, they do. Now, anyway. There's been a lot of deregulation of that business, so . . .

CABINET SECRETARY

You know what would be a great show?

ME

What?

CABINET SECRETARY

The office of a cabinet secretary. Be hilarious. The things that go on. People would love it. What do you think? Is there a show in that?

CUT TO:

INT. THE GRILL – DAY

A busy Los Angeles lunch spot.

SFX: Cell phone chirps.

Everyone in the restaurant instinctively checks his own phone. So do I, which is a good idea, since it is my phone that's beeping. That's the strange thing about cell phones: the ring seems to come from everywhere at once.

    I answer.

    MY AGENT (V.O.)

      Hi!

    ME

      Hi!

    MY AGENT (V.O.)

      So. Anything?

    ME

      Not yet.

    MY AGENT (V.O.)

      Well, don't panic. Just have a nice lunch and
      keep loose.

    ME

      Okay.

    MY AGENT (V.O.)

      Have a salad. You need the roughage.

    ME

      Excuse me?

    MY AGENT (V.O.)

      Physicalize the process. Pretend you're con-
      stipated. Relax. Eat some fiber. Don't panic.

Then, gradually . . .

ME

I'm eating, here.

MY AGENT (V.O.)

I'm just saying don't push. I'm just saying let it come naturally.

ME

And then when it does, we'll point to it and say, 'Is there a show in that?'

FADE OUT.

AUTUMN: 'I APPLAUD YOU'

FADE IN:
FLASHBACK SEQUENCE
Years ago, we wrote a tratment for a television series. This was an unusual thing to do. For some reason, it's considered eccentric for writers to *actually* write. We're supposed to pitch ideas verbally – go into the network president's office and *act passionate about the project*. But that has always seemed vaguely humiliating to us.

So our agent sent the treatment to a network, and before we knew it we were sitting in the office of some kind of network vice president.

OPTICAL EFFECT DISSOLVE TO:
INT. NETWORK VICE PRESIDENT'S OFFICE
– DAY
We are holding tiny bottles of expensive water and sitting on a soft leather sofa that is both oversized and slippery,

so that it's impossible to sit without sliding slowly off the cushions. It's an infantilizing piece of office furniture. My bottle of water sweats tiny droplets onto the arm, which pleases me in a petty way.

The vice president sits facing us. She smiles mirthlessly. She taps the treatment.

NETWORK VICE PRESIDENT

This is hilarious. *Hilarious*. We loved it here. Didn't we?

She turns to her staff. They nod and smile robotically.

NETWORK VICE PRESIDENT (CONT'D)

So . . .

ME

So . . .

NETWORK VICE PRESIDENT

Tell me about the show.

ME

Well, it's all right there in the treatment.

NETWORK VICE PRESIDENT

Yeah, but I thought the reason you wanted to come in was to *describe* the show. Isn't that why you came?

ME

Not really. We thought *you* wanted to see us, because you liked the treatment.

NETWORK VICE PRESIDENT

I didn't *like* the treatment. I *loved* the treatment.

ME

Great.

NETWORK VICE PRESIDENT

Great. But pretend you *didn't* write the treatment.

ME

Why would we do that?

NETWORK VICE PRESIDENT

I just want to get a sense that you're *passionate about the project.*

ME

But ... I mean ... we *wrote* a treatment.
Isn't that passionate enough?

NETWORK VICE PRESIDENT

But that's just writing. I like talking.

OPTICAL DISSOLVE TO:

END FLASHBACK SEQUENCE

What she wanted, of course, was a pitch. Which we don't
do.

We're fairly unique that way, actually. Most writers
prefer to pitch an idea before they write it, but in our
experience, this leads to difficulty.

The whole point of writing a treatment – or, better yet,
writing an entire script – is that there's very little confusion left about what, exactly, the show will be about and
who, exactly, the star or stars of the show will be, and
what, precisely, is or is not funny about it.

But when you pitch a show, you pitch into the wide
blue sky. You pitch the general idea, the concept – whatever that means – and you naturally smooth the sharp

edges and tailor the pitch to the involuntary reactive facial muscles on the face of the highest ranking decision-maker in the room. It's almost impossible not to. A pitch is like a performance by a raggedy subway clown. He just wants you to love him and toss him some change.

So the network hears what it wants to hear: that your show will be perfect for an actor they have a deal with; that it will concentrate on family life, snugly fitting into an open 8:30 PM slot; that its point of view will be single people, or urban dwellers, or blue collar, or married with childrens, or whomever the target audience is for that network, on that night, that week.

But you go back to your office, mysteriously forgetting the shabby desperation of your pitch. You start writing the idea that was in your head before you started talking to the impassive face of the network executive, before he or she started grinning slightly, before the first laugh, before you made the sale.

And in the ensuing weeks – and sometimes months – between the sale of the script based on the pitch (which usually takes place in October or November) and the actual writing and delivery of the finished draft (sometime in January or even early February), the difference between what they bought and what you sold becomes enormous.

The easiest way to explain the system is by describing when, exactly, a writer gets paid and for what.

If you pitch an idea to a network and they like it, they'll order up a script and pay you for that.

Once you turn in the script, they'll ask you to address

a set of concerns – they call these 'notes' – and you'll get another small check when you deliver a second draft.

The network usually orders more scripts than they need to produce, so after you've turned in your script, you have to wait a few weeks, or months, to see if they want to produce your script. This is called a 'pilot order,' and it comes with another juicy check.

You now have to hire a director, assemble a cast, and produce the pilot, all under the helpful supervision of the network and the studio. When this is done and delivered, usually sometime in April, you get another small check. And you wait until May, at which point the networks decide which old shows they still want, which shows they don't (see above), and which pilots they're going to order to series.

It's quite simple, actually, but we make it simpler. We write a script, usually over the summer, finish it in early autumn, send it out to the various networks, and hope that they want to buy it. No pitching, no back-and-forth notes, just writing and reading. To us, this has always seemed like a more sensible approach for all involved. If they like the script, they simply make it, without all the uncertainty and the waiting, and without the irritating flurry of small checks to cut. But to some in the business – certain *network executive* types – our system has a whiff of arrogance to it. *Take it or leave it*, we seem to be saying. (Well, not *seem*, really: that's exactly what we *are* saying.)

That's the way a couple of writers with big studio deals have always done it, anyway. But times change.

CUT TO:

INT. MY OFFICE – DAY

The phone rings. It is . . . well, you know.

    MY AGENT (V.O.)

      Hi.

    ME

      Hi.

    MY AGENT (V.O.)

      So.

    ME

      So.

    MY AGENT (V.O.)

      I'm trying to tell from your tone of voice
      whether or not you're wallowing in self-pity
      about how hard development is, but you
      haven't said enough yet for me or my assis-
      tant to tell.

    ME

      Your assistant?

    MY AGENT (V.O.)

      He listens in on every call I make. That's the
      only way he'll learn the business.

    ME

      Hi.

    MY AGENT (V.O.)

      But he's not allowed to talk.

    ME

      Oh. I thought young agents got their start in
      the mailroom.

MY AGENT (V.O.)

The *mailroom*? Why the mailroom? Who gets mail?

ME

I just thought—

MY AGENT (V.O.)

This is a *telephone* business. He learns by listening.

ME

Listening to clients?

MY AGENT (V.O.)

No, listening to *me*.

ME

Oh, see, I thought—

MY AGENT (V.O.)

You've got a meeting at [my agent mentions a big network] next week.

ME

But I don't think—

MY AGENT (V.O.)

Sorry, it's all set up.

ME

Oh. Okay.

MY AGENT (V.O.)

Did you see how I did that?

ME

Did what?

MY AGENT (V.O.)

I wasn't talking to you.

SET UP, JOKE, SET UP, JOKE

CUT TO:

We are at a professional crossroads. Our past series were entirely self-generated. That is to say, we sat in a room and stared at each other long enough until we had an idea and a script. The more popular and savvy approach is first to *ask* the networks what they might be interested in, and especially, which actors they have already put under a contract called a 'holding deal.'

You're then doing something called *developing for talent*, which means, simply, that you're coming up with a show for an actor who the network not only likes but is paying to sit around and be *available*. The word *talent* in this context simply means *actor and/or actress*. It doesn't mean *talented*. It's just a noun, interchangeable with the word *mammal*.

The problem with developing for talent is that it's not quite as soul-satisfying as creating from whole cloth. And the truth is, somewhere between coming in to the office at eleven, and leaving at three, we kind of have a tiny little kernel of an idea that we'd like to flesh out. If it were up to us, we'd just write the thing like we always have.

CUT TO:
INT. CAMPANILE RESTAURANT – DAY
Lunch with a couple of network executives.

    EXECUTIVE #1
        So . . . are you guys going to write another
        pilot or . . .

EXECUTIVE #2
    . . . you know, we've got some great talent at
    the network . . .
EXECUTIVE #1
    . . . some *terrific* talent . . .
EXECUTIVE #2
    . . . some talent with actual *talent*.
ME
    Well, obviously, we're not ruling anything out.
EXECUTIVE #1
    Of course.
ME
    I mean, we're *available*.
EXECUTIVE #2
    Gotcha.
EXECUTIVE #1
    So you're willing to develop for talent?
ME
    Of course.
Executive #2 reaches across the table and grabs my
arm.
    EXECUTIVE #2
    (deeply, with great feeling)
    I applaud you.

CUT TO:
When they say *I applaud you* they mean *not so stuck up
now, you arrogant shithead fuckfaces, are you?*

CUT TO:

INT. MY OFFICE – DAY

Later. The phone rings.

>MY AGENT (V.O.)
>
>Hi!

>ME
>
>Hi. And hi to your assistant.

>MY AGENT (V.O.)
>
>You're spoiling him! Look, I just got off the phone with the network. I don't know what you said at that lunch, but they're in love with you.

>ME
>
>Yeah, well, about that . . .

>MY AGENT (V.O.)
>
>You've been thinking, right?

>ME
>
>Right.

>MY AGENT (V.O.)
>
>You're not sure you want to develop for talent anymore, right?

>ME
>
>Right.

>MY AGENT (V.O.)
>
>So?

>ME
>
>Well, how do we get out of it?

>MY AGENT (V.O.)
>
>Get out of it? Why would you want to get

out of it? Look, they'll send over some tapes,
you watch them, if you like someone, great,
if you don't, too bad.

ME

But what if we don't like any of them? What
if the talent they've got holding deals with
sucks?

MY AGENT (V.O.)

In other words, what if the earth is round
and the sun is bright orange?

ME

Basically.

MY AGENT (V.O.)

Then I tell them that you're *available but not
interested*.

ME

What happens then?

MY AGENT (V.O.)

Usually, they go nuts and offer you double
the money.

ME

Oh.

MY AGENT (V.O.)

Why do you worry so much?

ME

Well, it's just that we actually do have kind
of an idea for a show . . .

MY AGENT (V.O.)

What? *What?* When did this happen?

ME

Well, we've been sitting around thinking, and there's an idea we've been kicking around about a guy—

MY AGENT (V.O.)

A *young* guy, yeah . . .

ME

A guy who suddenly discovers that his dad—

MY AGENT (V.O.)

His *young* dad, yeah . . .

ME

Do you want to hear this or not?

MY AGENT (V.O.)

I do, I do. Really. Pitch away.

ME

You know what? Forget it. We'll just write the thing and send it to you.

MY AGENT (V.O.)

And you'll watch the tapes, right?

ME

No way.

MY AGENT (V.O.)

Be realistic.

ME

No.

MY AGENT (V.O.)

You only have nine months left on your deal.

ME

Then I have nine months to keep being

86

unrealistic, right?

MY AGENT (V.O.)

That wasn't where I was going with that.

ME

Look, give us a month or two to write this
one. Let's just see how it goes. If it works,
and they buy it, then fine. If not . . .

MY AGENT (V.O.)

Then you'll watch the tapes?

ME

Yes. Then we'll watch the tapes.

MY AGENT (V.O.)

I applaud you.

CUT TO:

Of course, there's talent and there's talent. And no one
around here is claiming to be above a little schmooze
now and then.

For instance:

For many years, I have spent the Christmas holidays
with family and friends on a tiny island in the Caribbean.
The resort is a fairly low-key affair, but there are a few
movie actors, a television star, a famous journalist, and
a few politicians among the annual visitors. We all ignore
each other cheerfully.

One year, however, a studio executive I know comes
with his wife. He wants to know why I haven't taken
advantage of our island setting (no quick escapes; no place
to hide) to buttonhole one of the actors and convince him

to do a television series. One in particular is said to be considering a return to television. All that remains, according to the studio executive, is someone to 'reel him in.' When I explained the logic underlying the concept of 'vacation,' he stared at me uncomprehendingly.

'I'm not here to do deals,' I said, looking away imperiously. 'This isn't that kind of place.'

'I know,' he said, nodding vigorously, 'that's what makes it such a great place to do a deal. You know, you have the place to yourself. *No one else is going to poach that guy.*'

One morning, at breakfast, certain events beyond my control (newspaper, sudden gust of wind) caused me and the actor to exchange 'hellos.' And not just hellos, but handshakes and friends-in-common and, ultimately, some cups of coffee, a chat about 'The Business,' some discussion of what television needs today, and finally a promise to have lunch next month in Los Angeles. In short, I schmoozed. I would like to deny it, but I can't. I schmoozed, and worse, while I schmoozed, all I could think about was, 'So this guy wants to do a television show, huh?'

The next afternoon, while I was sitting by the dock waiting for the evening boat to arrive, the television executive catches up to me. He sits down in the chair next to mine, takes a sip of his rum punch, and shuffles around a bit.

I don't turn around. I know what he is doing. He has seen me talking to the actor, and he is grinning triumphantly. His is grinning, if it's possible, audibly.

'Nice work today,' he says, devil-in-my-ear.

'I'm sure I don't know what you mean,' I huff.

'C'mon,' he drawls, taking the pineapple slice out of the drink and biting it right to the peel. 'You cornered the guy,' he says, lips smacking around the pineapple, 'and you did the deed.'

'Oh, *that*,' I say, with a dishonest shrug, 'I was just saying *hello*. We have *friends in common*, you see. It wasn't *business*! It was just a friendly *hello*.'

'Yeah. Right.'

'Look, I'm on vacation, okay? What kind of loser schmoozes people on *vacation*?'

'No, no, I'm not criticizing,' he says. 'I was impressed. It was pretty slick.'

'Well,' I say, chilly and offended, 'I don't come all the way out here to do *business*, okay? If I wanted to do that, I'd be in Hawaii.'

A moment passes. We sip our drinks.

'It *was* pretty slick,' I say.

'Absolutely,' he says, raising his glass. 'Happy New Year.'

One more story to prove that we're not inflexible artistes:

A few years back, a local television station broadcast an exposé of some popular local restaurants. With hidden cameras and undercover reporting, they revealed that some of the most popular Los Angeles restaurants are guilty of some of the most unsanitary practices.

Waiters were secretly filmed licking their fingers and nibbling from plates that were about to be served. Salad tossers were caught sneezing into their hands and then tearing lettuce. Chefs were taped inadvertently knocking cigarette ash into stockpots.

The town was transfixed. In a city as scattered and scatterbrained as this one, few events manage to capture the collective attention. Fires, floods, riots, and earthquakes are the usual unifiers. Now we can add *E. coli in your tagliatelle al formaggio* to the list.

'People are going nuts over this thing,' an agent friend of mine said. I was sitting in his glass-lined office waiting to go to a Dodgers game and the conversation turned, as it did everywhere in Los Angeles that month, to the restaurant exposé. 'I've eaten in a bunch of those restaurants. And you know what? The food was good. I say, if you enjoy it, that should be enough. Some things you don't want to see being put together. Some things you're better off not knowing.'

I looked out of his silent glass office, onto the great bullpen of the agency. It was a scene out of a Bosch painting: assistants were scurrying around, agents paced wildly, screaming into headset telephones. The whole office was in the throes of its normal, everyday panic attack.

'Sort of like, you should just enjoy the movie or the television show. But no one should ever see how one is prepared,' I said, gesturing to the chaos beyond.

He stared out into the bullpen. 'Christ, yeah,' he said.

'If people only knew what we have to do to put a project together, they'd throw up and never stop.'

In the wake of the exposé, the local health board swung into action. All over town, restaurants began sporting large plastic cards in their windows, official issue of the health board, with a letter grade in bright blue. The grades go from an 'A' (which, presumably, means that you have the guarantee of the County of Los Angeles that no matter what you order, you won't get dysentery) to 'C' (roughly, 'You eats here, you takes your chances').

For a few tense weeks, everyone in town was doing the same thing: we'd cruise slowly by our favorite restaurants, praying for an 'A' in the window. Or, at the very least, a respectable maybe-it's-just-a-case-of-a-slightly-not-cold-enough-refrigerator 'B.' In a city obsessed with rankings and ratings, with who's-in-who's-out, the plastic cards with the big blue letters cut right to the heart of things.

'But last week,' the agent says, 'my wife and I went to a local sushi restaurant. We'd gone there a million times. Didn't think anything of it. We go, sit down, have some hamachi, some neguro, you know. *Sushi*, right? Then, we're leaving, I look down, and against the window, *way down there*, is the Board of Health grade. Guess what it was?'

'B?' I guess.

'Nope. It was a "C." I'm like, "Holy crap, my wife and I just ate 'C' sushi." I mean, "C" pizza, *okay, maybe*, it's hot, you know, and heat kills everything. But "C" sushi?'

'Yeah, I'm not sure about "C" sushi.'

'So my wife and I spent the night making each other vomit.'

'Wow. Really? How? Did you watch the *Something's Gotta Give* DVD?'

'No, we—' He stops himself, then laughs mirthlessly. 'Funny. Our feeling was, better safe than sorry. But the upshot is, from now on, we're strictly "A" restaurants. For *everything*. Actually, I think they should rate food shops, too. And shoe stores, you know? All that trying-on-and-off and other people's feet all over the place. And gyms. I mean, you're naked in those places with *other people*.'

It's time to get to Dodger Stadium. It is axiomatic in Hollywood that anything really important can only be discussed at the very last minute. It's the same principle which dictates that contract negotiations will break down irretrievably at six o'clock Friday afternoon, only to be revived an hour later, when everyone is hungry and cranky enough to settle. It is also what leads people to begin to reveal incredibly crucial bits of information just as the parking valet pulls up with their car, or, worse, while on the car phone, to say 'The most important thing to bear in mind is . . .' or 'They're offering you the sum of . . .' just as they head into a canyon where cell coverage is spotty.

'Look, we represent a piece of talent that's got a network relationship.'

What he means is, a network has just signed a giant

deal with a certain actress to star in her own half-hour comedy show.

'Who?' I ask.

He tells me the name of an actress who has recently declared during a television interview that she communicates with creatures from outer space. She has also, according to certain press reports, been in and out of drug rehabilitation several times. These things, though, don't really matter. Only one thing does.

'Is she funny?' I ask.

He shrugs. 'Not really. I mean, I don't think she's ever done comedy.'

'So she's crazy and she's not funny.'

'Right.'

I think about this for a minute.

'But she's got a deal,' he says. 'So are you interested? Please say "yes," because I already told them you'd take a meeting.'

'Not interested,' I say without pausing.

'She's A-list, I'm telling you.' He leans in, intensely.

I immediately picture this actress standing outside the studio gates, eyes drooping in drunken half-sleep, wearing a bright blue 'A' around her neck.

'Sorry,' I say, 'But A-list isn't what it used to be.'

Of course, we don't always say 'no' to those kinds of things. When you're applauded as much as we've been, you learn that taking a meeting with a *piece of talent* is the easiest part of development.

A few years ago, at the studio's behest, we met a very

talented actor who was interested in doing a half-hour television show. He's a funny guy: nimble, smart, with a hugely expressive face, and not too handsome – not handsome at all, really, which is perfect for comedy. Good looks tend to let the air out of any comic situation. Comedy relies on a certain amount of dire jeopardy for the main character, and if you're beautiful, how much trouble can you really be in? Because even after slipping on the banana peel, or waking up in a hotel room up next to a hooker with your wife on her way up from the lobby, or losing the suitcase full of cash for your boss's bail, if you've got great teeth and terrific breasts and cheekbones like tiny moons you're not really in much of a jam. You're beautiful. You'll figure it out.

Well, this actor wasn't beautiful, which made us interested in him in the first place. So after an hour or two of shooting the breeze and getting to know each other, *establishing a relationship* – you're hip to the lingo by now, right? – the three of us shook hands and parted, the actor back to his movie set, and the two of us back to our office to decide if we wanted to think up a series for him.

An hour later, the phone rang. It was the actor's manager. He wanted to know if we had any objection to having another guy, a friend of the actor's, coming on board as a producer.

'A producer of what?' I asked.

'Of the show. We want to attach him as a producer.'

'*Attach* him to whom?'

'To *you*. To the *show*.'

'We'd be happy to consider him for our writing staff. Send us his material.'

'But he can't write. He's not a writer.'

'Then what is he?'

'He's a producer. He *puts things together*. He *arranges elements*.'

'Still don't get what he does,' I said.

'He *facilitates*.'

'We don't need a facilitator. I mean, we write it. Your client acts it out. We get somebody to film it. What else is there?'

'This guy is real creative, I'm telling you. He's a terrifically creative person.'

'Can he write?'

'He's not a writer.'

'Then what is he?'

'He's a producer. He's attached and he's a producer.'

Let me tell you a story that I heard a few weeks ago:

A big television network signs a major Broadway star to do a series. This happens quite often, actually: the rigors of stage work – and the ability to charm an audience – are ideal training for a star of a half-hour comedy. So with the star suitably dazzled by flattery and woozy with gold fever, the network searches around for a writer.

They're looking for *auspices*, to use the industry term, which, like most industry terms, is neither accurate nor wholly literate. *Auspices*, around here, means not just a writer, but an über-writer – a guy, in other words, who will not only create a series and write the pilot episode, but who will also executive produce the resulting – one hopes – enormously enriching hit.

Hollywood almost always has two or three ways of describing the same job, each imprinted with its own little status DNA. There's no real difference, for instance, between a *cinematographer* and a *director of photography*, except that the former probably gets paid more money. Actors can be described as a *wonderful piece of talent*, an *element*, and, at the very top, *a creative force*. And a television writer is sometimes a *unique comic voice* then, if lucky, becomes a *writer/producer*, which, if everything works out, evolves into *show-runner*, until, finally, the six-figure *auspices*, as in: *We will pay a lot for a show produced under that writer's auspices.*

To be at the *auspices* stage of a career, for a television writer, is a little like being a 'made guy' in the mob: you're trustworthy, you're solid, and you have blood on your hands. 'What we need to find for you,' agents will tell a hot actor client who is considering a gig in series television, 'are the appropriate *auspices* to best serve your wonderful *creative force*.'

On with the story:

So the network finds some pretty impressive auspices – a guy with a hit show already on the air – and sets up the deal. The actor is thrilled (the guy writing his show – excuse me, under whose auspices the show will be produced – is the network's prize guy) and the writer, who is already rich, is on the brink of becoming *seriously* rich. Jerry *Seinfeld* rich.

Unfortunately, he can't write. He's awful. His scripts are unfunny, childish stacks of paper, with stories so conventional they're almost confusing, and jokes so flat you almost can't distinguish them from the stage directions. How this tiny talent of a man came to such worldly success is an example of the efficiency of the Hollywood economic model. You can get anybody to rewrite anything. Or, as the network executives like to say, 'We can always get somebody to make it *good*. What we need is somebody to *make* it.' A few years ago, this guy wrote a lousy, though professionally competent, script. All of the hackneyed elements were in place: setting, female lead character, pseudo-sexual tension – right out of the software program, SitCom 1.0. Not a lick of it was funny, of course, but that didn't bother the network. 'We can get somebody to plug the funny in,' they said.

So the show limps onto the network's schedule in the winter, sticks around until the following autumn, gets a few additions to the cast ('We can always plug some funny person into the cast,' I can hear them saying) and emerges as a late-blooming hit.

But the guy still can't write. But with a hit on the air and millions of dollars in the bank, he's forgotten that. All he knows is, 'Hey, look at me! I'm not just a writer! I'm auspices!'

So, over the holiday weekend, the guy writes the script for the Broadway actor. Early the next week, he gives it to a writer friend of his, to whom he has promised a staff-writing job.

'What do you think?' the writer asks his friend.

His friend has a choice: if he tells the truth, the writer may be so furious that he takes back the job offer on the spot; if he opts for mindless flattery, the writer may actually give the script to the Broadway actor *as is*, queering the deal, also resulting in his friend's unemployment. It's a classic Hollywood ethical dilemma: either choice ends up in a job search. The friend chooses the middle path, the typical Hollywood way – he tells the writer a half-truth.

'It's pretty good,' he says, slowly, hoping to be let off the hook. 'I mean, it's a first draft, right?'

'Nope. It's fine the way it is. At least, I think so. Don't *you*?'

'Oh, yeah. Yeah,' says the friend, mindful of his house payments. 'It's just that, I mean, shouldn't the network see it first? Maybe give it a second pass or something? You know? Like a polish or something? Just tweak it a little? Here and there? You know?'

The writer does not give the script to the network first. And he does not 'tweak' or 'polish' it at all. Instead, he flies to New York, presents the whole muddled, jarring, monotonous raft of drek to the Broadway actor, in his dressing room, between the matinee and the evening performance.

By the time his plane has landed at Los Angeles airport, the Broadway actor has read the script, called his agent, pulled out of the deal, and issued a press release announcing his decision to 'concentrate on the arena of feature films.'

'The dumb ass showed him the script,' the network executive fumed. 'He actually thinks he's a good writer. I tried to tell him, "You're not a good writer." I said, "You don't *have* to be a good writer. We can *get* somebody to be a good writer for you." And the guy says to me, "Then why have me do the show at all? If you can get somebody to write it, what do you need me for?" So I told him, "We like your auspices."'

Which, when you think about it, makes a certain kind of sense.

It used to be that television was the movie actor's boneyard. If you were getting old, hadn't had a decent movie part in a while, but drank too much or gambled too much or maybe just had to put some kids through college, you were what people around town would call 'ready for television.' As in: 'Is so-and-so ready for television?' 'Yes, but he doesn't know it yet.'

These days, with many actors on television commanding salaries in excess of $500,000 per episode – for, if we all don't have enough resentment stored up against them, a paltry twenty-two episodes per year – and even then, some of them get something called a 'producer credit,' which is a license for mischief, well, it isn't a question anymore of being 'ready for television.' Some of the biggest names in Hollywood are raring for television. Some of them, in fact, are circling the studio in makeup.

That's the cynical reason why so many actors are 'ready for television.' The other reason is less colorful, but equally true. Most of the feature films being made these days are insufferable, ghastly little pieces of retreaded crap, with funny dialogue so unfunny, and scary dialogue so unscary, that television actually benefits from the comparison. So when an actor weighs the higher salary and the better material against the small step down in prestige . . . you see where I'm going with this.

A few years ago, when we were casting a television series, the network wanted us to meet with an aging movie star with an eye toward casting him in the lead role.

This happens quite often in television. Movie stars, especially *former* movie stars, regularly become 'available' for television shows, usually around tax time. It's an alluring gig for an actor: a steady paycheck, six months off, short work days . . . and still in the public eye.

The actor that we met with, though, wasn't your regular long-in-the-tooth, graceful-exit type. He was one of the biggest movie stars of all time. Twenty years ago, he was, in fact, the biggest box-office attraction in the world. Now, he was broke and in our office trying to pretend that he wasn't broke and he wasn't asking for a job.

How he got broke was a simple case of making a gajillion dollars a year, but spending a gajillion and one. It's a remarkable sight, watching an actor spend money. They don't so much *spend* it as *fling it in all directions*. It cascades out of every orifice, to the assistants and the nannies and the household staff and the lawyers and the guy who helps you charter a plane. Get divorced, and the cost of everything doubles. Get divorced again, and you'll discover what ancient Chinese mathematicians called the 'ruinous curve.'

The meeting was heartbreaking. As much as we wanted to give him the job, we knew we couldn't. The few people who had worked with him in the intervening swan-dive years all gave us the same advice: run. He's crazy, they said. He refuses to work for days. He's late. He's impossible. He argues with the director. He reblocks the cameras. He'll accuse you of trying to murder him. And worst of all, he punches people. Writers especially.

'If you cast him, you'll have to get a *side agreement*,' my agent said.

'What's a side agreement?' I asked.

'It's an understanding. A legal understanding between you and the studio. It means that if the guy hits you and you don't want to come to work anymore, they can't sue you for breach of contract.'

'Do you think he'll really hit us?'

'You're a writer, aren't you?'

'Then forget it,' I said. 'Who needs this kind of aggravation?'

There was a pause on the line.

'Well,' my agent began, slowly, 'before we get all "forget

it" about this, let's remember that the guy is a *huge* star. A *gigantic* star. He's not just a piece of casting. He's a piece of business. He's an *element* to the show.'

'Meaning?'

'A star like that could make your show a hit. Do you really want to say "no" to that kind of opportunity?'

'Well . . .' I said, wavering.

'Look,' my agent said, 'what's so great about being easy to work with? I'm *horrible* to work with, and I'm doing okay. Everything has its drawbacks. Some stars make you hire their idiot friends on the writing staff, some insist you donate to their crackpot charities, some drink, some bang underage kids, and some . . .' My agent paused, winding up, '. . . and some even want to *write*. So in the grand scheme of things, what's a couple of swings from a former box-office sensation and star of your *hit* television show?'

I think about this for a moment.

'He can't hurt us, though, right?' I ask. 'What are we talking about? A black eye? Swollen lip?'

'Honestly? As your agent and legally enfranchised representative, I'm ethically bound to inform you that the guy was, in fact, an amateur boxer. What we are talking about is something on the order of a broken jaw or burst ear drum.'

In the end, we passed. The actor was charming in the meeting, but then, he was an actor. He's *supposed* to be charming in the meeting. A television show, even a hit television show, isn't worth having your teeth knocked out.

'You're crazy,' my agent said. 'You'd have a hit on your hands.'

'Sorry,' I said. 'I like my teeth and my jaw and my ear drums.'

'You still don't get this business, do you?'

We don't. So we start writing.

BEGIN AWFUL, CLICHÉD MONTAGE:
(MUSIC UP: AN UP-TEMPO HIT)
1. We're hard at work, staring at a large bulletin board on the wall . . .
2. Our assistant takes shorthand as we pace and gesticulate wildly . . .
3. The printer spits out pages and pages of dialogue . . .
4. We sit at a table, marking up a script with red pens . . .
5. Silence. Lost in thought. Then, one of us says something, and the other bursts out laughing . . .
6. Moonrise over Los Angeles . . .
7. A darkened studio lot . . . PUSH IN TO REVEAL: One office light flickering . . . PUSH IN TO REVEAL: A finished script in the copying machine . . .

(MUSIC CROSSFADES OUT; SFX: COPYING
MACHINE CROSSFADES IN)
END AWFUL, CLICHÉD MONTAGE
FADE OUT.

Another phone call, Monday, 2:36 PM

'Are we all on the line?'
  'You've got Josh.'
  'Delia here.'
  'Jamal here.'
  'Trish.'
  'Eli.'
  'Hi, it's Beth.'
  'Okay then, I'll put Josh on the line.'
  'Hi, everyone.'
  'Hi Josh!'
  'How's Montreal?'
  'Great! Some really great new comic voices.'
  'That's great, Josh.'
  'Josh, hi, it's Delia. I'm new here, so I may be breaking the whole "protocol thing," but I've seen some of the tapes we've been getting from Aspen and Montreal and I really think there's something in the new wave of ironic man-boy comics reflecting on childhood. And I think we

should be developing some kind of project along those lines.'

'*That's a good point, Delia.'*

'*Thanks, Josh.'*

'*Okay, so what are we doing here?'*

'*Did you get a chance to see the material we sent you?'*

'*Yeah.'*

'*Well, we've put a call into him to give him some notes and feedback . . .'*

'*Okay.'*

'*. . . And we wanted to get your thoughts first.'*

'*Okay.'*

'*Okay.'*

'*My feedback is I don't get it.'*

'*. . . "don't get it," okay . . .'*

'*I mean it's like stories and gossip and I don't know what else. Is it darkly comic and I just don't know it?'*

'*I think that's a fair response, Josh.'*

'*What do you think, Josh?'*

'*I guess my concern is that we may be dealing with some form of satire.'*

'*Yeah.'*

'*Yeah.'*

'*And that really is not going to work for us.'*

'*And what's the jeopardy here for this guy? Does anybody really care if he gets his hit show on the air? Is anyone in America going to root for this guy? It just seems elitist and pointless and . . . just a second, I've got the room service guy here . . . hey, I wanted the glass bottle of Evian, not the large plastic one.'*

'?*Que?*'

'The GLASS bottle. Not the PLASTIC bottle. The PLASTIC gives you cancer.'

'Josh?'

'Yeah?'

'Do you think we should just shut this project down?'

'No, no. Wait a sec. Right! Glass! Right! No, no, we shouldn't shut it down. Just make the guy more like someone who people might like and respond to. Not so many stories. More jeopardy. More sex, maybe.'

'There's no sex in it at all, Josh.'

'Good point, Delia.'

'But don't you think we should focus our notes on the main character?'

'Yeah. Focus on making him a more believable, likable, heroic . . .'

'. . . passionately committed to his art and craft . . .'

'. . . striving . . .'

'. . . attractive . . .'

'. . . everyman.'

'Right.'

'Right.'

'Right.'

'That's him on the other line right now. Should we all get on, or . . .'

'Delia?'

'Yes?'

'Do you want to take this by yourself?'

'Sure!'

'Okay, he's all yours. 'Bye.'

''Bye.'

''Bye.'

''Bye.'

'You've got Delia. Go ahead.'

'Hello?'

'Hi!'

'Hi.'

'Thanks so much for getting back to us so quickly. First, I just want to introduce myself. I'm Delia and I'm sort of taking over for Beth and Eli and helping out while Josh is in Montreal.'

'Are you Trish's replacement?'

'No, actually, the whole team has been reorganized, and we're now broken up into "pods" that cover the various projects we have in development.'

'I'm in your pod?'

'Right!'

'Okay.'

'So first, let me just say, "Welcome to my pod!" No, seriously, I'm just so happy to be working with you. Anyway, I know how you writers all hate the whole "getting notes" thing and I totally agree with you. It's the worst part of my job. What I want to do is work with writers and just kind of brainstorm and be creative and really contribute to the process. You should know that I'm really picky about the projects that I work on and when I work on something, I'm totally about that one

*project and just, like, so fucking passionate about it it's
scary.'*

'Okay.'

'Great. So really our one basic note is, can the whole
story start faster?'

'I'm sorry?'

'And is there some way to make one of the characters
a little more reflective of the ironic man-boy voice?'

'I beg your pardon?'

'Let me send you some tape on that.'

WINTER: 'HAPPY HOLIDAYS'

At Christmas time Hollywood denizens suspend their usual adult-sized greed for the simpler, more innocent greed of a child.

Hollywood – climate and religious diversity notwithstanding – is a Christmas kind of place. And if one doesn't send out hundreds of Christmas cards (sample message: 'May the Joy of the Season Warm You and Your Family. A donation in your name has been made to an Important-Sounding-Charity.'); send gift baskets of tiny, inedible muffins; and in general behave as if one day's generosity can somehow mitigate 364 days of cruelty and selfishness; well, then, just how does one expect to succeed in this town?

In what I now realize were the Fat Years – years, that is, when we had a television series in production – my office was a Christmas Wonderland. Baskets and baskets of fruit and whiskey and horrible-tasting Italian cookies jostled for space among the flowers and useless crystal items. The office reception area was thronged with messengers and delivery men bearing gifts. One year, a large television network sent out large red footlockers filled with candles and doodads and, oddly, a terrycloth bathrobe. (The robe I gave to my assistant: the thought of emerging from the shower, naked and dewy moist, and wrapping myself in something that came from the president of a television network was just too creepy.)

In fact, most of the gifts end up with the assistants. Hollywood, after all, is a truly Christmas kind of place. Here, it's the thought that counts. We don't care if the baked goods are stale, if the wine is obscure, if the bathrobe is creepy, or if the last thing we want is a weird crystal toe-shaped thing with the Time Warner logo on it – we just want it, wrapped and delivered. We just want to know that we're loved, even if only by a corporation's computer-generated people-we're-doing-business-with-this-year list.

So when Christmas rolls around, we celebrate in two distinct ways.

The first way, as I've mentioned, is by sending elaborate gifts to people who do not need them. Every agent, studio executive, network president, and entertainment lawyer sends every writer, actor, agent, studio executive, and network president they're in business with (or *want* to be in business with) some kind of gift – food is popular, as are small electronics.

The second way is by firing all of the low-level employees, forcing them off the payroll and onto state-sponsored unemployment benefits for the *two weeks* between Christmas and New Year's Day, and then promising to rehire them the first Monday in January. A hugely profitable television production company did just that last year, claiming that they needed to 'make economies to compensate for our increased level of executive gift-giving.'

In other words: we're doing so much business that we can barely afford to send everyone presents. See you in January.

My partner and I have always given out Christmas bonuses to our employees. Cash bonuses, by the way, and fairly generous ones, we thought.

In the years that we have a series in production, the bonus pool gets quite large – split unevenly among six or seven office assistants. In the years that we're developing a new series, the office is quite small: just us and our colorful-but-surly assistant.

Earlier this month, our assistant made it subtly clear that his annual bonus was too small. He made a few veiled comments like: 'My annual bonus is too small,' and, 'If it's going to be that small again this year, please just don't bother with it at all. It's too humiliating to take it to the bank.'

Stung, we had a conference. Our assistant, though cranky and reflexively disrespectful, is in fact an excellent assistant: his typing skills are impeccable, his shorthand is efficient and complete, and when we're in production, he runs a flawless team of sub-assistants. He is, in short, a valuable employee.

And at Christmas time, when our offices overflow with ridiculously extravagant food baskets and disconcertingly personal gift items, it seems churlish not to spread the largesse around a bit. My partner suggests a healthy increase in our assistant's annual bonus.

'But I gave him my massage oil,' I whine.

Still. Maybe a cash increase. We've been very busy these past months writing two scripts, each one of them requiring long days of fast typing.

'And I also gave him the lavender eye mask we got from the guy who fixes the fax machine,' I say, holding out.

In the end we decide to give our assistant what is known in Hollywood as a 'bump.' As in: 'We're bumping up your bonus.'

On bonus day, we handed the envelope to our assistant, who instantly put it aside and continued typing the script.

'Aren't you going to open it?' I asked.

'After I finish this,' he said airily. 'I don't want to lose my motivation to do a good job.'

'Open it,' I said in a low, irritated voice.

'After I finish typing—'

'Open it!' I barked.

He opened the envelope. The Christmas bonus check – now adjusted north by a zero – tumbled out.

He looked at the check. Barely a flicker crossed his face.

'What happened?' he asked. 'Did you get visited by three ghosts last night?'

'It's in recognition of all that you do,' I said, with distinct irony.

'Well,' he grumbled. 'Thanks, I guess.'

'You're welcome,' I snapped.

'Merry Christmas,' he sneered.

'Happy New Year,' I snarled. 'And hurry up with that goddam typing.'

The Christmas spirit, when it comes, always has a dollar sign attached.

DISSOLVE TO:

INT. MY OFFICE – DAY

I'm sitting at my desk, looking out the window. A large truck has just driven up outside, laden with enormous-looking wrapped gifts.

A delivery man hoists one or two onto his shoulders, and heads for our office door. He leans in.

DELIVERY MAN

    Is this the *Frasier* office?

MY ASSISTANT

    That's next door.

DELIVERY MAN

    Thanks.

    The door slams shut. The phone rings.

MY AGENT (V.O.)

    Hi. Happy Holidays.

ME

    Merry Christmas.

MY AGENT (V.O.)

That's like your subtle way of saying 'I'm not Jewish,' isn't it?

ME

No. A lot of my Jewish friends say 'Merry Christmas.'

MY AGENT (V.O.)

That's like your subtle way of saying 'A lot of Jewish people like to pretend that they're not around Christmas time,' right?

ME

Are you calling me anti-Semitic?

MY AGENT (V.O.)

Of course not. Of course not. You're just defensive. Your problem is that you only hear what you *want* to hear.

ME

Actually, my problem is that I *never* hear what I want to hear, even when what I want to hear is being said.

MY AGENT (V.O.)

Listen, I'm not your shrink. I just called to say that I'm heading out for the . . . *holidays* . . . and that I'm sending you a little something.

ME

Gosh, thanks.

MY AGENT (V.O.)

Simmer down. It's not a gift.

ME

Oh. What is it?

MY AGENT (V.O.)

It's the comprehensive list of all of the half-
hour series that all of the networks are developing for next fall.

ME

Why on earth would I want to look at such
a thing?

MY AGENT (V.O.)

Find out what you're up against for the
fall. See what the competition is. You know,
info.

ME

It sounds depressing.

MY AGENT (V.O.)

You know what's more depressing? Ending
up next May with no shows on any network.
I suspect then that you'll look back on the
time you spent perusing the development list
with a warm fuzzy feeling.

CUT TO:

My agent, as always, is right. The development list arrives,
it is sixty-three pages long, and it is depressing. As I read
it, Bob Cratchit-style, I see more vans pull up outside my
door, all laden with gifts, all going to other people, people
with shows on the air. A production facility I have never
used, in a part of the San Fernando Valley I have never

visited, inexplicably sends me a cardboard desk calendar. I give it to my assistant, who receives it with what looks like pity in his eyes.

The development list is a purely-Hollywood document: the list is based on unequal parts rumor, lies, and incontrovertible fact. No network wants its competitors to know its precise plans for the following year, so the list takes on the complexity of a Le Carré novel. Some projects are clearly lies told by the network ('Harrison Ford Sitcom Project'); some are lies told by a studio ('One of seven thirteen-episode commitments'); some are last year's projects that no one knows the status of ('Writer doing feature film; may be avail. '06'); and some are outright ludicrous ('our little production company – twenty-two episode commitment').

Still, if only one-half of each network's development slate is factual, the news is very grim indeed. Each network, by my count, is actively developing fifteen or so series. And each network, by my count, only needs four.

CUT TO:
INT. MY OFFICE – DAY
We are sitting around watching CNBC, the financial news channel, to see if anyone is trying to purchase the studio where we work, or the network we want to order our show. Outside, the steady parade of gifts to other producers continues.
SFX: phone rings.
    MY AGENT (V.O.)
        Did you get the list?

ME

  I did, thanks.

MY AGENT (V.O.)

  And?

ME

  It looks bad.

MY AGENT (V.O.)

  Why?

ME

  Look at all of the stuff they're developing.
  It's going to be hard for our script to cut
  through all of that, don't you think?

MY AGENT (V.O.)

  Actually, I don't think it will be. I sent your
  script out last week and they bought it this
  morning. You're making a pilot.

ME

  What? *What?*

MY AGENT (V.O.)

  I thought to myself, 'Hey, should I tell him
  ahead of time, or should I just send it out
  and tell him later?' Isn't that what I said?

MY AGENT'S ASSISTANT (V.O.)

  That's what you said.

MY AGENT (V.O.)

  Ultimately, it was an easy decision to make.
  I mean, there's so much about this business
  that you can't handle, I thought I'd spare you
  the *agita.*

ME

Well, thanks. But then why did you send over
the development lists?

MY AGENT (V.O.)

Because even now that you're making a pilot,
you're still a long shot for a series order. And
if you get to make twenty-two episodes,
you're still likely to—

ME

Get cancelled in May. Got it. Thanks for the
lesson.

MY AGENT (V.O.)

That, my friend, is my *Christmas* present to
you. Merry Christmas.

ME

Happy holidays.

CUT TO:

I am meeting a woman for dinner at a local restaurant.
I arrive a bit early, take a seat at the bar, and order a
drink. Two seats down, also waiting for his date, is an
actor I know vaguely. We wave to each other and strike
up a conversation.

'How are you doing?' I ask.

'Pretty well,' he says. 'How about yourself?'

I tell him that my writing partner and I have just had
our pilot picked up by the network. I tell him that we're
happy to be casting and producing, because sitting around
thinking all day is a difficult process. We throw out a lot

of ideas, we sit in silence a great deal, and ultimately, we miss the structured day and organized existence that having a series in production provides.

He nods sympathetically.

'Well,' he says, 'I haven't worked in about a year. And at first, all that unstructured time kind of drove me nuts. All of those empty, aimless days spent waiting for auditions. The isolation. The sitting around. I really thought I was going to go insane. But lately, I've come to enjoy it.'

'Really?' I ask. 'How are you keeping busy?'

'I've been doing a lot of research lately,' he tells me. 'On the internet.'

'About what?' I ask.

He takes a sip of his beer, and then says, matter-of-factly: 'About the healthful effects of drinking your own urine.'

I'm a writer, obviously, and not a scientist. I can't speak for the healthful effects of anything, much less my acquaintance's new beverage choice. But I can say, without hesitation, that in all the times I've felt bored or out of sorts, had a show cancelled, been stymied for ideas, felt useless and without direction – felt, in other words, the way a writer in Hollywood feels when he's not asleep, I've never been tempted to, shall we say, sample my own wares.

'Hollywood,' someone once told me, 'is divided into two camps. In one camp are the people you have to wait for, the people who come up with the ideas and write the scripts. The writers, in other words. They're the "wait-fors." Nothing can happen and no one gets hired until they write the script. And in the other camp are the people who wait for the writers. Those people are actors. Also known as "waiters."'

The irony, of course, is that while they're waiting for a part to come along, most actors work as waiters. And while we're waiting for inspiration to strike, most writers are eating in restaurants. I like to think that if most actors were better waiters, we writers would get our food faster and get back to work sooner. And no one would be doing 'research' on the internet.

CUT TO:

INT. OFFICE – DAY

We are sitting with our casting director, who has brought a long list of actors who might be right for our show.

> ME
>
> (pointing to a name)
>
> What about him? How old is he?
>
> CASTING DIRECTOR
>
> His agent tells me that he's a very fit sixty.
> But I did a little checking and discovered that
> he was a contract player at MGM in the fifties,
> which makes him—
>
> ME
>
> Ninety. He's ninety.
>
> CASTING DIRECTOR
>
> His agent swears to me that he's a fit sixty.

ME

How old is his agent?

CASTING DIRECTOR

Twenty-seven.

ME

Next name.

We go to the next name, a big star.

CASTING DIRECTOR

This guy is perfect for you. He's funny, he's the right age, he's available and interested in television. He'd be a home run.

ME

Great. Let's bring him in to read for us.

CASTING DIRECTOR

(chuckling)

Oh, he won't *read*. He's too big. He'll *meet*. He'll come in and *meet*.

ME

Umm, okay. Then why don't we get him a script and see if he's interested in the part, and if he is, then let's meet.

CASTING DIRECTOR

Are you offering him the part?

ME

How can we offer him the part if we haven't even met him yet?

CASTING DIRECTOR

Well, he won't read the script unless it comes with an offer.

ME

But how can we offer him a role unless we at least meet the man?

CASTING DIRECTOR

(in a bored monotone)

He won't meet unless he reads and he won't read unless you offer it to him first. He's *offer only*.

ME

What about some guys who aren't *offer only*?

CASTING DIRECTOR

You don't want them. Trust me. Anyone worth casting won't read the script, won't audition, and probably isn't interested.

CUT TO:

It turns out, our casting director is telling the truth. The few agents who call to tell us that their clients have read our script, love it, and want nothing more than to audition for us this afternoon do their clients no service. We are instantly suspicious, and by the same stupid reasoning that leads you to reject a romantic partner who likes and respects you for one who lives to make you unhappy, we too reject the willing, easy, professional actor for the unattainable, super-sexy *offer only*.

The problem, as always, is money. Ordinarily, the studio fronts the money to pay the entire production tariff. In the local patois, they 'deficit' the production, meaning that they agree to lose tens of millions of dollars up front, in exchange for the potential bonanza that exists if the show lasts long enough to go into reruns. 'Long enough' is currently defined as roughly five years.

It's in the long-term interests of the studio to keep costs – and the financial risk – down. But since it's in their short-term interest, unfortunately, to supply the buying network with a dazzling product, it's a good idea to cast big stars in the show. Big, expensive stars.

Occasionally, for a big star – or what we call *a major piece of talent* – the network will agree to kick in a little money. But only as a last resort. And they'll never tell you until the very last minute.

The result is something out of Pinter: two cheapskates trying to avoid picking up the tab for dinner.

CUT TO:
INT. NETWORK PRESIDENT'S OFFICE – DAY
There are eight of us in the room. We are all reviewing the casting possibilities for our show.

> NETWORK PRESIDENT
>> I like a lot of these names.
> ME
>> Me too. Especially . . .

I name one of the actors on the list.

> NETWORK PRESIDENT
>> I like him a lot.
> ME
>> Me too.

CASTING DIRECTOR
Me too.

NETWORK VICE PRESIDENT
Me too.

STUDIO PRESIDENT
But he's expensive.

STUDIO VICE PRESIDENT
Very expensive.

NETWORK PRESIDENT
Is that a problem?

STUDIO PRESIDENT
I don't know. Is it?

NETWORK VICE PRESIDENT
For an important project like this, we should
be prepared to pay top dollar, right?

STUDIO VICE PRESIDENT
We?

NETWORK PRESIDENT
Whoever.

STUDIO PRESIDENT
The point is, can we afford him?

NETWORK PRESIDENT
I don't know. Can we?

STUDIO PRESIDENT
I don't know. Can we?

CUT TO:
INT. OFFICE – FOUR DAYS LATER
The phone rings.

MY AGENT (V.O.)

Hi. I just got off the phone with the network.
They're not so pleased with the way the studio
has handled the casting. The word they used
was *obstructionist*.

ME

Well, we've been going after some pretty
expensive names.

MY AGENT (V.O.)

I know. Listen, everyone wants big names, no
one wants to pay big money. It's the same
everywhere. I want Armani Le Collezione; I'll
pay for Armani Exchange.

ME

It's the *offer onlys* that have hurt us.

MY AGENT (V.O.)

Why are you bothering with *offer onlys*?
C'mon! Do you have any idea how many
great actors there are living in seedy apart-
ments in the Valley, making their way from
urine-smelling passageways to late-model
Chevrolets for a drive to the day-old bakery
on Magnolia and Burbank?

ME

What?

MY AGENT (V.O.)

Like it? I'm taking a creative writing class at
UCLA Extension.

ME

  Great.

MY AGENT (V.O.)

  Relax. You'll find somebody. And it'll be
  somebody affordable.

ME

  What if we don't?

MY AGENT (V.O.)

  Then we tell everyone that the studio was
  obstructionist and you leave in a huff.

ME

  Can we afford to leave?

MY AGENT (V.O.)

  I don't know. Can you?

ME

  I don't know. Can I?

MY AGENT (V.O.)

  What?

ME

  I mean, didn't you tell me that there were no
  more deals anywhere?

MY AGENT (V.O.)

  I don't know. Did I?

Pause.

MY AGENT (V.O.)

  Look, do you want to take some meetings
  around town at different studios? Just kind
  of a meet-'n'-greet situation? In case there's
  some money for deals next year?

ME

No. I want offers. No meetings. I'm *offer only.*

MY AGENT (V.O.)

(chuckling)

You kill me. You really had me going there. Bye-bye.

ME

I'm serious.

MY AGENT (V.O.)

Bye-bye.

ME

I mean it. I'm totally—

SFX: Click. Dial tone.

CUT TO:

About ten years ago, on a Hollywood soundstage, an actor threw such a tantrum that the next day he felt compelled to apologize to an assembly of the cast and crew. This is not as rare as it sounds: most actors, after a big meltdown scene, like to follow it up with a big apology scene. In this case, the actor made a tearful show of it, abjectly throwing himself on the mercy of a group of people who owed him their livelihood. (Surprise! They forgave him!)

But he wound up his speech this way: You gotta understand, he said, what I've been through this month. A friend of mine has cancer, my girlfriend and I are having problems, and *I've been through an earthquake.*

He was referring, of course, to the Northridge quake,

which devastated parts of the San Fernando Valley, felled a freeway overpass, and killed over fifty people. But to this actor – and I suspect he's not the only actor who felt this way, nor, for that matter, the only person in the entertainment industry who felt this way – everything is a personal thing. Earthquake? *My* earthquake. Holocaust? *My* holocaust. As Daffy Duck once shouted to Elmer Fudd, trying to keep him from pulling the trigger, 'I'm different! Pain hurts *me*!'

CUT TO:

INT. MY CAR – DAY

SFX: phone beeps. I answer.

    MY AGENT (V.O.)

      Hellloo.

    ME

      Hi.

    MY AGENT (V.O.)

      Congratulations! I hear you have an excellent cast!

    ME

      Thanks. We're pretty happy with the way it turned out.

    MY AGENT (V.O.)

      See? What did I tell you? It's impossible, it's too expensive, it can't be done, and then, suddenly, it's done.

    ME

      That's certainly how this turned out.

MY AGENT (V.O.)
I have a thought for the title of your show.
ME
We have a title.
MY AGENT (V.O.)
I mean a better title.
ME
What is it?
MY AGENT (V.O.)
Call it 'Here They Come!'
ME
I don't get it.
MY AGENT (V.O.)
It's about a young guy and his dad, right?
Who are also friends? Get it? Growing up I
had a friend and we were inseparable. And
when people saw us coming, they'd say, 'Here
they come!'
ME
I'm not sure America will get it.
MY AGENT (V.O.)
But *I'll* get it.

CUT TO:
We have employed the same assistant for several years.
Besides being lightning fast with shorthand, he's also a
devoted student of astrology, and he has acquainted us
with the astrological concept of the 'void.'

Simply put, a *void* occurs during the absence of any

astrological force. It means, essentially, that you are free floating. A void, by its very definition, is indifferent – the stars are neutral for however long the void lasts, which can be a few minutes or a couple of days.

After my partner and I spend a desultory afternoon of smoking and gossiping and staring at each other, we look forward to our assistant's ability to explain our laziness away with an astrological alibi: my trine is in his house, he's in retrograde, or (my personal favorite) something called *moon wobble*. The point is, it's not our fault.

'How're we doing?' one of us will ask. 'Are we in a void?'

And he will fix us with a withering gaze and answer, 'No we are not. Astrologically speaking, you *should* be working efficiently. And anyway, a void is what you bring to it.'

From the Hollywood perspective, a void is the worst possible situation. The heavens arrayed against you is preferable to their indifference. It is better to be on the top of everyone's enemies list – they know who you are! They can spell your name! At lunch they all talk about how awful you are! – than to be unknown, undespised, unspecial.

'I truly believe,' an agent told me once, 'that my grandparents were spared the horrors of Nazi Germany because God wanted me to revolutionize the talent representation business.'

Now *that's* special.

Worse, because 'a void is what you bring to it,' there

are no tricks or blessings you can rely on to get you out of trouble, and no negative heavenly force you can use as an excuse when you fail. A void is the astrological version of having a script with no actor or director attached, of having a show with no big-name star or network commitment, of having to rely, at the end of the day, on the merits of the material. Nothing could be more terrifying.

CUT TO:

INT. MY OFFICE – DAY

We are having a cup of coffee. In less than an hour, we're holding the first reading of our pilot script. This is the event that sets the tone for the rest of the production week. The stage will be filled with executives from the network and the studio, with the actors and their agents, with various other personnel, and, finally, with us.

> ME
>> (to my assistant)
>> How're we doing?

> MY ASSISTANT
>> (quietly)
>> We're doing very well.

> ME
>> What does that mean?

> MY ASSISTANT
>> It means that halfway through the reading,
>> we'll be void.

> ME
>> No!

MY ASSISTANT
Remember: a void is what you bring to it.
ME
That's what I'm afraid of.
MY ASSISTANT
(encouragingly)
And you're bringing a great script and a ter-
rific cast. You'll be fine.
ME
I guess so. Besides, just for a little extra good
karma, as I turned left on Crenshaw Boulevard
this morning, I gave the homeless guy who
hangs out there five bucks.
MY PARTNER
You did? Uh oh.
ME
Uh oh what?
MY PARTNER
I gave him twenty. You know what you have
to do now, don't you?
I nod. I dash out to my car and zoom down Crenshaw
Boulevard waving fifteen dollars out the window. Karma?
My karma.

FADE OUT.

A 'Concept Meeting', Tuesday, 2:45 PM

'*Should we wait for Josh?*'

  '*I'm Josh.*'

  '*No, I mean the other Josh. The head of the division.*'

  '*Oh.*'

  '*Oh, right.*'

  '*Oh. Well, I think that Josh isn't going to be at this meeting. This is just a concept-y kind of meeting.*'

  '*Concept-y?*'

  '*I think what Delia means is that we're just going to give our feedback on the pages up to now, and maybe think of ways to platform some of the moments better.*'

  '*Just a chance to take a beat.*'

  '*Right. Take a beat.*'

  '*Just to take a beat.*'

  '*Thanks, Eli.*'

  '*First, let me just say that everyone in the pod is thrilled with this project. Really.*'

  '*It's my favorite project of the entire pod. And that*

includes drama hours and some reality business, too.'

'Gosh, thanks.'

'No, thank you. For bringing us this really edgy project.'

'You know, we're always saying that we want more edgy stuff, more stuff that's challenging to our audience, and this certainly is it!'

'Well, thank you.'

'And I think what we like the most about it is that it's dark and kind of inaccessible.'

'Inaccessible?'

'You know what I love about it? I love the whole "aging failure scrambling for money" aspect.'

'I like that part too, Delia.'

'Me too.'

'Me too.'

'That's still there? Because I was trying to . . .'

'I guess I want it to get even darker'

'Darker?'

'Yeah. I mean, I'm getting the idea that you're holding back a little, you know . . .'

'Well, I'm trying to keep it likable.'

'Don't!'

'Don't?'

'No! Go for it! Get as dark and as edgy and as unlikable as you want. Really. That's what's working for me.'

'I agree with Delia.'

'I agree with Josh about agreeing with Delia.'

'Delia?'

'Yes, Eli?'

'Is there a sense – and I'm just throwing out an idea here – is there a sense that some of this could be even more dark, and more edgy?'

'I think I agree with you, Eli.'

'Because he could really push it, and we could easily dial it back if it gets too far.'

'Of course.'

'Of course.'

'Of course.'

'So . . . you want me to be even sharper?'

'Yes.'

'We're saying that we love the area you're in, in terms of tone.'

'Tonally, we love it.'

'Love it.'

'So don't worry about being likable?'

'But don't tell anyone I said so! They'll take my executive's license away!'

'Hahahahahahahaha.'

'Hahahahahahahaha.'

'Hahahahahahahaha.'

'You know, I don't even think of myself as an executive. I think of myself as a writer, but . . . you know . . .'

'A writer who runs a pod?'

'Right.'

SPRING: 'THE MIDDLE DISTANCE'

FADE IN:
One of the more comforting aspects of Hollywood is how dependably it lives up to its clichés. You are, in fact, only as good as your last picture. You will, in the end, learn that you've been fired from the parking lot attendant. And it is, despite sprawling over two mountain ranges, a freshwater river, miles of coastline, three telephone area codes, and a knot of concrete freeway, a very small town.

A friend of mine filmed a television pilot recently, and he and his partner, the director, take it to one of the market research facilities here in town to be focus-grouped. Thirty or forty scientifically assembled partici-pants (culled from the local tourist traps) wait in the broiling sun for an hour or two until they are led into a dark room with a one-way mirror and told to watch the pilot, after which they will be asked for their responses, and after that presented with a crisp twenty-dollar bill. These drowsy, hungry, grouchy folks with a lifetime of unfulfilled longings hold the future of a million-dollar piece of film in their mitts. I often wonder why they always give them the money *after* the session, and not before, to cheer them up a bit, but this is the way they've always done it so this is the way they do it still.

The testing goes quite well. We call it 'testing' the pilot around here because of the grim clinical connotations of the word. In my friend's case, the focus group enjoyed the show, giving it a 'will watch' designation, which is about the highest possible rank. They were unanimously negative, however, on one point: a particular actress they all despised with equally high intensity. In the guided discussion that followed the screening and the questionnaires they filled out, the participants, to a person, remarked on the general badness of this particular actress. They all hated her. They hated her face. They hated her voice. They hated her body. They hated her totality. At one point in the show she is standing next to a box of newborn puppies. They decided that they also hated the puppies, which was a market-testing first: puppies, kittens, and children in wheelchairs always test very well.

The problem was that the actress was married to the director. And the director was behind the one-way mirror, listening to America tell him how repellent his wife was. Also behind the mirror were representatives from the studio that produced the pilot, the network that bought the pilot, and the writer, none of whom had the courage to so much as steal a sidelong glance at the director, who, presumably, stared straight ahead into the middle distance,

with that vague, abstracted smile people get on their faces
when they don't know what else to do.

CUT TO:
INT. MY OFFICE – DAY
The phone rings.

 MY AGENT (V.O.)
  Congratulations!
 ME
  For what?
 MY AGENT (V.O.)
  Just congratulations. Are you excited?
 ME
  About what? Congratulations for what?
 MY AGENT (V.O.)
  You shot a fabulous pilot that the whole town
  is talking about.
 ME
  We did?
 MY AGENT (V.O.)
  Don't you hear the buzz?
 ME
  We're too busy for buzz.
 MY AGENT (V.O.)
  Well then, let me clue you in. The buzz is
  very good on your show. And you know what
  they say about the buzz.
 ME
  What do they say about it?

MY AGENT (V.O.)
　The buzz is never wrong.
ME
　Sure it is. I can't tell you the number of times
　I've heard great things about a show only to
　have it flop terribly.
MY AGENT (V.O.)
　You're a nervous person. You're a doom-
　sayer. Do you have TMJ?
ME
　What's that?
MY AGENT (V.O.)
　It's a muscular disease you get in the jaw from
　clenching it too much during bouts of stress.
　I'll bet you have it.
ME
　(unclenching jaw)
　Do not.
MY AGENT (V.O.)
　It's sad, really. You're on the cusp of a big
　success. The buzz doesn't lie. The buzz is never
　wrong.
ME
　What about shows that have great buzz
　around town, but then nobody in America
　watches?
MY AGENT (V.O.)
　Usually by then the buzz has changed, only
　nobody noticed.

ME
Oh.
MY AGENT (V.O.)
Of course, I notice everything.
ME
Oh.
MY AGENT (V.O.)
I'll call you if the buzz changes.

CUT TO:

The story of the director and his actress wife was told to me at lunch one day. Our bored, apathetic waiter overheard the story and identified himself as one of the participants in the focus group. It seems that he and his other flat broke actor friends hang out at the Farmer's Market, a local tourist attraction, waiting to get picked for focus groups. Whoever gets picked buys two pitchers of beer with the $20.

I ask our waiter about the actress that his group loathed with such certainty. He tells me that he actually thought she was pretty good, but that he had once taken an acting class with her and she had been a 'total bitch,' so he turned the group against her. I ask him if he doesn't feel a little bit guilty, since the network, following the focus group, insisted that she be recast and the pilot re-shot without her. He shrugs. 'I dunno,' he says, 'I figured it was okay since the show sucked so bad. I mean, I knew it was never going to last more than six episodes.' I ask him how he knew that. 'The buzz, man,' he says, shrugging for the ninety-seventh time, 'the buzz on that show just totally *bit*.'

This is a small town. No matter where you are, you can hear the buzz.

CUT TO:
INT. MY OFFICE – DAY
The phone rings.

>MY AGENT (V.O.)
>Hi hi.

>ME
>Hi.

>MY AGENT (V.O.)
>I just thought you'd like to know that [my agent mentions the name of an actor who's in a new half-hour television pilot] just flipped his car and has checked himself into rehab.

>ME
>Ouch.

>MY AGENT (V.O.)
>Ouch and not ouch. Production has been postponed for six months, which means he's out of consideration for the fall. Which means that there's another slot available for a new show.

>ME
>Oh.

A pause.

>MY AGENT (V.O.)
>Like yours.

>ME
>Did we get an order?

MY AGENT (V.O.)

You didn't get one this morning? Wow. I was pretty sure you'd have one by now.

ME

Why?

MY AGENT (V.O.)

Because I have a dear friend – someone I've known a long time – someone I *go back with*, you know? And, his show has been scuttled.

ME

Why?

MY AGENT (V.O.)

They hated the pilot. What can I say? He's a dear, dear friend. A close personal friend. He's like a brother to me. But he can't write for shit.

ME

Oh.

MY AGENT (V.O.)

I mean, the man gives you *nothing*. *Nothing on the page*. And for some reason it's hard to really see that until you actually make the pilot.

ME

Well, since we're exchanging gossip, I hear that [I mention the name of another project] has hit the wall too. Apparently the pilot tested terribly.

MY AGENT (V.O.)

Not true. Not true at all.

ME
  No?
MY AGENT (V.O.)
  No. You know what that is? That's a vicious
  lie, that's what that is. Jesus, this town is sick.
ME
  Gee, sorry.
MY AGENT (V.O.)
  In the first place, the script was moving, pas-
  sionate, and, may I say, magisterial.
ME
  Okay.
MY AGENT (V.O.)
  And in the second place, the network loved
  it. They're in love with it. And it tested fine,
  for your information. There were some con-
  cerns with male audience appeal, of course –
  there always are. And some of the female
  demos didn't really respond to the arena, but
  you know what? They hated *Seinfeld*, too.
  And *Friends*. Both shows tested for shit.
ME
  Okay. Okay. *Okay.*
MY AGENT (V.O.)
  So stop spreading lies. Stop smearing your
  filth all over town.
ME
  I'm *sorry*. Okay? Man, what is it? Are you
  friends with the guy?

MY AGENT (V.O.)
    He's a client.
ME
    Oh.
MY AGENT (V.O.)
    What? You thought you were my only client?

CUT TO:
INT. HAVANA ROOM – NIGHT
I'm drinking with a friend. He has a show on the air and is waiting to hear if the network is going to cancel it. I am suddenly struck by the thought that one year ago, I was in his shoes. And now, one year later, I'm the one with a hot pilot, warming up on the sidelines, ready to go.

That afternoon, he got a call from his network's president. It was intimated, but not said outright, that his show is about to be cancelled.

Because our pilot is for another network and because the failure of his show can in no way – even in the remotest possible sense – help our show, and because I was at his wedding, and because in the past, when I've been depressed about something or needed someone to talk to he has always been available and ready to take me out for a drink or snap me out of it, when I put my hand on his shoulder and say *You got screwed, my friend, it was a good show you did and it deserved better*, what I actually mean is *You got screwed, my friend, it was a good show you did and it deserved better*, rather than what I usually mean, which is *Does this event help me in some way? I need to think about this for a moment.*

Of course, he cannot claim to be shocked. In the previous week, my friend's show had drawn what is known as a 'nine share,' which means that 9 per cent of all television sets in use at the time were tuned to his show. As I'm writing, that's a bad number. You strive for double-digits at the very least.

MY FRIEND

    I don't get it. We were doing so *goddam well*.

ME

    (gently)

    But last week you pulled a 'nine.'

MY FRIEND

    I know. That's what I mean. We were doing
    so *fuckin' well*.

ME

    (tough-love style)

    C'mon, buddy. You got a 'nine.' That's . . .
    well, I'll be honest, that's a shit number. You're
    lucky they didn't yank the show in the middle
    of the broadcast.

MY FRIEND

    Yeah, except every week they've been calling
    and telling us how much they love the show,
    and how happy they are with the numbers.
    Last week, when we bagged an eight share,
    they sent us all fruit baskets.

CUT TO:

My friend had committed a classic Hollywood error. He had received a fruit basket without grasping its subtext. To him, the gift card that read, 'Congratulations! We're thrilled with the ratings!' meant, roughly, 'Congratulations! We're thrilled with the ratings!' What it really meant was something closer to, 'You got a nine! Pack your things!'

He can be forgiven his confusion. With the explosion of new networks and the proliferation of cable stations, the expectations for network ratings have diminished considerably. Fifteen years ago, a twenty or twenty-five share would have indicated a moderate-to-low success. Today, that same number connotes a huge runaway hit.

Expectations, however, have not diminished so much that a nine means anything other than pretty instantaneous cancellation. In general, I've found, the problem with diminished expectations is that they never seem diminished enough.

The network management, though, will be relentlessly cheerful and encouraging right up until the moment that they cancel you. And it's almost impossible – or, more truthfully, it's almost impossible *for me* – to tell the difference between a genuine fruit basket and an impostor fruit basket.

The strange thing about the American television ratings is that for all of the attention paid to the *national* ratings, it's the *local* ratings that really count for big money. There are roughly one hundred and fifty television markets in the US – that is, regions that have three or more local network television affiliates. And because the major national networks only provide about nine hours of programming a day (two in the morning, one in the afternoon, four at night, and one or two during late night), that leaves a juicy fifteen hours for the local stations to fill with reruns, old movies, used-car ads, and general crap.

All of this is pretty irrelevant background information, frankly, but it does illustrate the hardiest of entertainment industry truths: the really big money is found in the most unglamorous places. In the feature film business, a Julia Roberts movie is great to have in your production pipeline, but its real value comes when you make every theater that wants to book it (or every international distributor that wants to sell it overseas) buy a couple of duds along with it. And in the television business, the primetime network shows are the loss-leading window-dressing baubles that attract the eyeballs that stick around for the reruns, old movies, used-car ads, and general crap.

But as much as I would like to have offered sympathy to my friend, I have a pilot in contention for the fall, and I am too wrapped up in my own numbers anxiety (not to mention daydreams of plush, early retirement) to offer much except to buy his drinks.

Besides, he's hard to feel too sorry for. He's a friend, of course, but friends are the people you see most clearly. And according to him, the network complained early on that his show wasn't funny enough and he rather arrogantly ignored them.

'So I told them,' he said to me over lunch one day, 'that I think jokes are *easy*. It's *easy* to be funny.'

'Really?' I asked him. 'It's always been kind of hard for me.'

'That's because your shows are *supposed* to be funny. They're like the filler between the good shows that are supposed to mean something.'

I would have felt insulted had I not been flattered. I have worked very hard to make our shows funny while avoiding 'meaning' anything. That, actually, is my working definition of 'entertainment.'

'Still,' I said, 'you could put in a few more jokes, right?'

'Aren't we all just *bored* of jokes?'

'I'm sorry?'

'What's so great about being funny? What is this obsession with funny funny funny all the time?'

'I wouldn't call it an *obsession*, really.'

'It's all just "set up, joke, set up, joke." I mean, just a string of hilarious one-liners? How easy is *that*?'

'Easy?'

My friend went on. 'I said to them. "Don't you want something different? Something that really breaks the cookie-cutter mold? Something *edgy*?"'

'What did they say?'

'They said they had that already. What they wanted was *funny*. And I told them that I don't do *funny*. I do *edge*. I do *meaningful television*.'

'And then what did they say?'

'They didn't say anything.'

'Oh.'

'I think I won them over.'

But of course, he didn't win them over. When they don't say anything, what they're saying is '*You're cancelled.*' But my friend didn't know that yet. He still thought he was doing fine. He's like a lot of people in Hollywood: they all want to do the marquee products; they all want to do the Julia Roberts movie; they all want to make the loss-leader. No one wants to do the filler. No one wants to be simply *funny*.

Except me. I know that it's the filler that pays the bills and buys the yachts and builds the houses by the sea.

CUT TO:

INT. MY CAR – DAY

I am driving to work. My car phone rings.

    MY AGENT (V.O.)

        Hi. Have you heard anything from the net-
        work? What have they said about your pilot?

    ME

        They called this morning. They said they're
        thrilled with it. They said it's a lock for the
        fall schedule.

    MY AGENT (V.O.)

        Oh no.

    ME

        I'm kidding. They didn't call.

    MY AGENT (V.O.)

        Don't do that to me. I'm plotzing here.

    ME

        It was a joke. Sorry.

MY AGENT (V.O.)
>Okay. Fine. Look, as long as they don't send you any fruit baskets, you're still in contention.

CUT TO:
INT. OUR OFFICE – DAY
A messenger appears at our door, burdened by three large fruit baskets from our network. We panic.
>I call my agent.

ME
>We're dead! They sent us fruit baskets!

MY AGENT (V.O.)
>What?

ME
>We're dead!

MY AGENT (V.O.)
>I'll call you right back.

SFX: hang up.
Moments pass. The phone rings.

MY AGENT (V.O.)
>I just spoke with the VP over at the network. He assures me that the network is truly happy with the pilot, and that the fruit baskets are actual fruit baskets.

ME
>They're really happy? Are you sure?

MY AGENT (V.O.)
>I'm sure. Enjoy the fruit.

CUT TO:

On the way home, I give the fruit basket to the homeless man who hangs out by the freeway entrance. This time, I think to myself, the fruit baskets were sent without sub-text. But next week? And the week after?

'Thank you, mister,' the homeless man says to me.

'Get used to it,' I mutter grimly.

The next day, my friend calls me up.

'It's official,' he says. 'We're cancelled.'

'Sorry to hear that,' I say.

'You know how it went down? This is classic. Get this: they call me up on Monday and tell me that they want to have a meeting this morning to discuss the creative direction and development of the show. For next season. And I said to them. "Does this mean there's going to be a creative direction and development of the show next season? Because I've been getting some pretty strong signals that we're about to be cancelled." And they're, like, "Are you kidding, we love the show, blah, blah, blah." So I'm thinking, okay, we're going to get to do a few more of these at least. So this morning I'm in my car, driving to the meeting—'

'The one they called, right?' I ask, just for clarification.

'Right. Right. The meeting *they* called. And my car phone rings. It's the network. Calling to cancel the meeting. Because they're cancelling the show.'

'What about the meeting?'

'Right! What *about* the meeting? What *about* the *fucking* meeting?'

'That they called.'

'Right! That *they* called.'

'Did you ask them?'

'Oh yeah. And do you know what they said? They said that on *Monday* they didn't think they were going to be cancelling the show, but that *today*, this *morning*, they changed their minds.'

'Today is Wednesday.'

'Right. *Right!*'

'What happened between Monday and this morning?'

'I *asked* them that. And do you know what they said? They said that the research numbers hadn't been fully crunched on Monday because the guy who crunches them was at his kids' soccer game or spelling bee or tonsillectomy or whatever-the-fuck, and when he got back the next day, he discovered that, statistically, we could never be more than a nine-share show. And he sent the network president an email that night – last night – to that effect, but that the network president left early that day to go to some fucking charity bullshit thing – what's the thing where your skin gets all hard and your face turns into a big toenail?'

'Scleroderma?'

'Whatever the fuck. Anyway, he's there until late, doesn't check his email until this morning, by which time I'm on the fucking 134 heading to his fucking office.'

'Wow.'

'Wow is right.'

A moment passes. I can hear my friend slowly calming down.

'Do you know who I blame?' he asks, quietly.

'The network?' I ask helpfully.

'No. Not the network. Those guys are just doing their jobs. No, who I really blame is *America*. I blame them.'

'You're mad at America?'

'Damn right. I gave them a meaningful, nuanced half-hour show and they just ignored it. Just goddam *ignored* it. Well, you know what? Screw them.'

'Screw America?'

'Damn right. From now on, I'm only going to do *funny* shows. You know, like the kind you do. I mean, *fuck* it. From now on it's just *set up, joke, set up, joke*.'

Which, again, I know he means as an insult. But I also know that he's a friend, and in Hollywood, you're not obligated to be happy for your friends' successes, or be disappointed in their failures, or even think they're very good at their jobs. In Hollywood, to be a friend, your basic job is to sit there, listen to their bitter complaints, and agree with them that *yes, everyone at the network is a fucking moron* and *yes, everyone at the studio is a cowardly bureaucrat* and *yes, your stuff is so much better than anything out there*.

Jerry Lewis, the Ur-Jim Carrey, once bid farewell to a nightclub audience with this heartfelt prayer: 'May all of your friends,' he intoned, 'be show business people.'

What he meant, I guess, is that show business people – or, in the earlier jargon, 'show people' and in the earliest jargon, 'carnival people' – have uniquely deep and satisfying friendships. As Frank Sinatra was once overheard saying to a close friend, 'I wish that someone would hurt your family so that I could find that person and hurt them back.'

A few years ago, when we were shooting the pilot episode of a new series, we asked a veteran comedy writer to help us out for a day. The term is 'punch up:' you invite an experienced vet to come to a run-through of your new show, then over a nice dinner and a good bottle of wine, hope that he pitches a dozen or so killer jokes and 'punches up' the script.

Although it may not seem like it to read this book, television writers form a loose but comprehensive web of friendships, and older writers, who are rich and bored and eager to help out, are sometimes the difference between a lackluster pilot that never becomes a series, and a hilarious pilot that makes it to air. This guy was one of the best, and we were excited to have him agree to help out.

'One question,' he said, 'before I get there.'

'Ask away,' I said.

'Who else will be working that day?'

I named a few of the junior-level writers. Then I named an older writer, a guy who's been around.

'Him?'

'Do you know him?' I ask.

'*Know* him? Yeah, I *know* him. I *hate* him. I *know* him and I *hate* him.'

'Oh. Will that be a problem?' I asked.

'Not for me,' the vet replied, ''cause I won't be there. Call me later, when he's gone.'

'But what did he do?' I asked, frantic. 'Why do you hate him?'

There was a long pause on the telephone line.

'Truth? I'm not sure. I can't remember.'

The only thing he remembered, naturally, was that he hated the guy. The other guy couldn't remember ever working with the old vet, and was completely bewildered by the feud.

Bewildered but philosophical: 'If the guy hates me, then he hates me. I never met him before in my life, but it takes a lot of integrity and discipline to hate a guy you've never met or worked with,' he said. 'And you gotta respect that.'

I am out having a drink with my best friend, an actor. He is telling me about the past television season, and how impossible it had been for him to get hired on a certain network.

'I couldn't figure it out for the longest time,' he says. 'I'd go on lots of auditions, have tons of call-backs, but in the end, they never hired me.'

I give him the it's-a-crazy-fuckin'-business shrug.

'But then I realized,' he went on, 'that it was always one particular network. Like I was being blackballed by someone in the casting department.'

'C'mon. You're being paranoid.'

'I'm serious. But not just *blackballed*. Blackballed with *extreme prejudice*, 'cause they'd call me in, then call me back, get my hopes up, and then bang, they'd pass on me. It was like someone out there really hated me.'

'Of course someone hated you. You're an actor.'

'Not just hated. *Hated* hated.'

I give him the it's-a-crazy-fuckin'-business-someone-always-hates-you-but-what-can-you-do-about-it shrug, which is similar to the basic it's-a-crazy-fuckin'-business shrug, except that it's delivered with a sad shake of the head.

'So I do a little research,' he tells me. 'I find out that the vice president of casting is a guy who was best friends with that girl I was living with when I . . . you know . . . *met my wife.*'

Met my wife is a sophisticated umbrella euphemism for a story that you can probably figure out yourself, in that it involves a guy, his girlfriend, and the woman who later became his wife. The story turns, as all love stories do, on issues of timing: when did *she* find out about *her*?

It turns out that the girl he was living with when he . . . you know . . . *met his wife* . . . had lots of friends in low-level jobs in the entertainment industry, friends who, in the intervening years, have acquired high-level jobs in the entertainment industry, and in one particular case, a high-level job in network television casting. And that guy, out of perverse and long-lived loyalty, is torturing my best friend.

'Wow,' I say. 'What are you going to do?'

'What can I do? I'm just going to wait it out, hope he gets bored, or hope that he suddenly realizes how bizarre it is to punish me for something that happened years ago.'

'Hmm. I guess that's all you can do.'

'Well,' he says, 'what did *you* do when you found out how much they hated you at the network?'

I look up from my drink. 'What network?'

My friend names the highest-rated network in American television.

'They hate me?' I ask.

'You didn't know?'

'*They* hate *me*?'

'You didn't know?'

'What did I ever do to them?' I ask in a tiny, childish voice.

'Maybe it's those stupid books you write, about how dumb they are. Where you write down all the stupid stuff they say.'

'But I make most of that up,' I shout. 'They *know* that, right?'

Then maybe it's because you never listen to their notes. Who knows?' he says.

'But I can't believe you didn't know that they hate you. It's kind of a famous feud.'

'It's *famous*?'

'Well, isn't it obvious? They never buy any of your shows. I can't believe this is news to you.'

'I've never been hated before. I've always been the *hater*, not the *hatee*.'

He gives me a it's-a-crazy-fuckin'-business-someone-always-hates-you-you-pathetic-out-of-touch-loser-I-can't-believe-you-didn't-know shrug, which is similar to the

157

basic it's-a-crazy-fuckin'-business shrug except that in addition to the sad shake of the head, his eyes are closed.

CUT TO:
INT. MEN'S LOCKER ROOM AT THE SPORTS CLUB LA – DAY
The Sports Club LA is one of the more glamorous Industry gyms. It also has two of the dozen-or-so squash courts in town, which is why I'm there.

I am dressing. A well-toned man with the locker next to mine has just come from the shower. He sees another friend a few lockers down. His friend is portly and balding.

> MAN
>> Hey! How are you?

> HIS FRIEND
>> I'm okay. You?

> MAN
>> Not bad.

The man stares at his friend.

> MAN (CONT'D)
>> Jesus, you've gained weight.

> HIS FRIEND
>> (ruefully)
>> Yeah, yeah. I know.

> MAN
>> No, I mean it. Like, what? Thirty pounds?

> HIS FRIEND
>> (slightly defensive)
>> Twenty-five.

MAN
  Still.
HIS FRIEND
  I had cancer. Didn't exercise for a while.
MAN
  Oh.
HIS FRIEND
  (moving off to the showers)
  Nice to see you again.
MAN
  You too. Let's have lunch sometime.
HIS FRIEND
  I'll call you.
They wave. His friend moves off.
MAN
  (muttering to no one in particular)
  He didn't have cancer.

CUT TO:
For all I know, of course, the guy really *didn't* have cancer. Maybe he just ate too much pizza. Still, his friend felt under no obligation to a) believe him, b) pretend to believe him, or c) simply ignore the extra thirty pounds. He did, though, feel obliged to arrange a friendly lunch.

Charitable organizations capitalize on this weird kind of friendship. Every two weeks or so, an invitation will come to the office to a dinner in honor of some Industry heavyweight. The strategy is simple: The Center for Unhappy and Misshapen Children will decide to honor the newly-installed chairman of a studio, not because the chairman has ever expressed the slightest interest or concern for the Unhappy and Misshapen, but because there are enormous numbers of people in town who are willing, for the price of a piece of leathery chicken and a pale yellow carrot (roughly $1,500 per person), to publicly express their friendship with the new studio chief. Or, failing that, there are larger numbers of people who are willing, for the price of a single-page ad in the dinner's program, to express their friendship and admiration for the boss ($2,000 for a black-and-white ad, $4,000 for color, $20,000 for the back cover). These ads almost always have identical copy – something like: 'To New Studio Head, Your passion and caring inspire us all, with much love, Person You've Met Only Once.'

We got suckered into this recently. We shelled out $1,000 each to place a similar ad in the dinner program for a charity dinner in honor of the CEO of the conglomerate that owns the studio where we work. 'Best wishes,' we wished the guy. It wasn't necessary to append the phrase, 'From Two Guys You've Never Met or Laid Eyes On.' That was implied.

What *wasn't* implied was the news, one week after the dinner, that the CEO had left the conglomerate that owns our studio for another conglomerate that owns another studio. So we were out two grand for kissing the wrong guy's ass.

Let me tell you a story:

Recently, the president of a large division of a large

studio was given his walking papers. Nothing personal, of course – the guy was good at his job (or, more accurately, as good as anyone else would be tasked with the same pointless responsibilities) – but the chairman of the studio had just installed a new president of the division under which the fired guy's division nested, and the new guy wanted to bring in fresh blood.

Usually, the new guy runs a bony finger down the organization chart and silently ticks off the names of everyone senior enough to gun for his job and fires them, thus ensuring that the new team running the studio has one powerful captain surrounded by terrified eunuchs. But firing people costs money – there are contracts, you see, and stock options – so the new guy has to be very careful to fire only those employees who pose an actual threat, by dint of their intelligence or courage or originality or some other personality defect, and not waste money on the drones.

So the old guy is out and he knows it. He's not bitter at all. Being fired, obviously, is proof of his value – if he wasn't good at his job, they would have promoted him. But he is more than a little broke. He has a house in the Riviera section of the Palisades (the best address in town, trust me on this one), a vacation place in Telluride, two kids at the Crossroads School, and a wife who has confused 'having a job' with 'writing a novel.' He needs a steady, fat stream of cash coming in to match the steady, slightly fatter stream of money flowing out, mostly to the American Express corporation and a mortgage banker specializing in something called 'jumbo financing.'

The financial ace up his tattered sleeve is a bushel of stock options that are, in our bubble-economy parlance, 'in the money.' So right after he gets his walking papers he calls up his old friend, the corporate treasurer, in New York. 'Hey, buddy,' he probably put it, 'you and I go way back, we're pals, our wives and kids know each other . . . I've got these options I want to cash in. I know you can't legally tell me exactly what to do, but I'd appreciate it, since we've been friends for so long, if you'd indicate to me if I should exercise them now, or if the rumors I hear are true and there's going to be a buyout of the studio, thus increasing their value tenfold, and making me a very rich man. A rich, retired man. What do you say, pal 'o mine?'

The story goes that there was a long pause on the line. And then the corporate treasurer said, 'My friend, I shouldn't tell you this, but just because you're you, I'll tell you unequivocally, that it doesn't matter at all.'

'So I should exercise the options today?'

'I'm telling you that it won't matter one way or the other.'

So the guy exercises his options. And it did matter one way or the other. The following Monday, a large media conglomerate announced a buyout of the studio, increasing the share price by a factor of ten, then, a few months later, by a factor of fifteen. Personally, I like to think that the corporate treasurer had the buyout agreement documents on his desk while he was telling his old friend, three thousand miles away, that it 'won't matter one way or the other.'

That's the way we operate out here. We're cruel, sure. But we're subtle.

So why didn't the treasurer tell his friend to hold on to his options? One possible explanation: it would be illegal to do so and corporate treasurers are notoriously honest.

Done laughing? Good. Let's get to the real reason he didn't.

He's mean. He's a mean, jealous guy and he didn't want his 'best friend' to be too much richer than he. A little richer, okay. A lot richer – and we're apparently talking in the tens of millions, here – not okay.

Also, he knows that in Hollywood behavior of this kind has no consequences. Those two guys, it should be noted, are still close friends. Sure, they might have hit a rough patch around, say, the time the stock price hit $108 per share (up from its quaintly respectable option price of $6) but they've worked through it, see. The definition of 'friend' is so elastic in Hollywood that it includes the definition of 'enemy.' This town is so small that everyone eventually brutalizes everyone else. We're like rats in a coffee can: nowhere to go but at each other.

Last month, for instance, the president of one of the top-rated large television networks was unceremoniously booted from his job. It was long in coming, we all thought. The network was starting to lose its luster: the old hits were running out of gas and the new season had been a tire-screeching car wreck of failures. Worse, his past success had made him arrogant and impossible to deal with, and at least two writers I know had named characters after him: in one cop show, his namesake was a gay cannibal serial killer; in another, he was a severely retarded little boy.

Still, when he was booted, they gave him something called a *golden parachute*, which means, roughly, that he has been paid handsomely to get out and get out quick. He got some cash and a production deal at the network, the standard industry goodbye for a worn-out executive. (If you grasp the logic underlying the decision to reward an executive who can't come up with any more hits with a high-priced production deal so he can try to come up with some more hits, then by all means come to Hollywood and seek your fortune. If not, stay put.)

But even with his savings and his parachute, we all knew that the guy's got a big house to pay for and expensive tastes. Worse, he has ambition. So instead of retiring quietly (and cheaply) out-of-state, he decided to try to make a go of it on his own, you know, to *put things together*. To *brainstorm creatively with the writers*. To *serve as a catalyst for disparate elements*. He's always thought of himself as *creative* and *not just one of those uptight executives*. So, he decided, *I'm going to be a producer*.

Before that could happen, though, he needed to mend some fences. You don't spend as many years in the big boy chair as he did and not piss a lot of people off. So he had to spend six days driving around town visiting the various writers who despise him, tearfully attempting to make amends. He is a smart guy, this former network president. He will have to attach himself to something. And somewhere in Hollywood there is a writer who has both forgiveness in his heart and a project that needs a guy who *facilitates*.

Mending fences isn't easy. It takes a certain talent. A couple of years ago, a young, aggressive talent agent – there are no other kinds, of course, but around here we still use the formal honorific – devised a brilliant trick to solve a thorny problem.

The ordinary back-and-forth efficiency of commerce in Hollywood is often blocked by pride. It's hard to believe, I know – the people who made *Boat Trip* have pride? The guys behind *America's Most Talented Kids* have pride? – but it's nevertheless true. We've all got a little place in this sticky spider's web, and it's important to keep up appearances. Small issues like 'who called whom first' and 'let's meet in *my* office; no, let's meet in *my* office' often sink entire deals. And because film and television projects always include three distinct and prideful elements (the star, the director, the studio, the network, the writer – pick any three) most of the time the business resembles a huge costume ball where everyone wants to dance, but no one wants to have to ask.

Which is where agents come in. This particular young, aggressive talent agent had figured out that if you place a call to one party, announce yourself as someone else –

someone, say, that the person you're calling has a stalled, bogged-down deal with – then, while you're waiting to be put through, call the *other* guy, announce yourself as the first guy, then link the two calls using the conference button on the phone, you can easily get two people who weren't going to call each other (unless the *other* guy made the first move) to talk, to discuss, and to eventually make a deal, preferably on a project that one of your clients has an interest in.

This trick only works because no one in Hollywood places his own phone calls.

What happens is this: Important Person tells Important Person's Assistant to call Down To Earth Me. My phone rings. My Down To Earth Assistant answers (not even the Down To Earth answer their own phones, of course) and is told that Important Person wants to talk to Down To Earth Me. I pick up my phone and say a cheery 'Hello, Important Person!' at which point Important Person's Assistant says, in a voice both bemused and pitiful, 'Just a moment. I'll put Important Person on the line.'

You can see, then, how easy it is to call someone on the phone and still make it seem as if they've called you. Because in Hollywood – and I'm not sure Hollywood is all that different from the rest of the world in this respect – it is far better to be called than to be calling.

The scariest words in the English language are, 'You don't remember me, do you?'

Well, maybe not the scariest. The *actual* scariest words are probably, 'The chef doesn't believe in printed menus, so I'll just describe what we're offering tonight,' but 'You don't remember me, do you?' is right up there.

I heard those words at a meeting with the president of one of the biggest studios in Hollywood. I had been presented the customary bottle of water, guided to the plush suede sofa, and just at the moment that the small talk puttered to a stop, he fixed me with a half-smile and dropped the bomb.

I didn't remember him. At all. But we're roughly the same age, so our paths could have crossed and double-crossed lots of times: school, college, film school, the early days of our careers – really, when you think of it, the past is filled with dozens (maybe even hundreds) of moments in which one is, to say the least, not at one's best. And those moments are preserved in *someone's* memory, like tiny buried stink bombs, ready to be dug up and exploded with a simple 'You don't remember me, do you?'

Think of the terrible possibilities: I'm the guy you threw up on in college. I'm the guy who was up for the job you eventually got. I was the guy answering the phones the day you decided to let the first guy who answered the phone have it. I was your waiter. Or, worst of all for someone who has worked in Hollywood for fourteen years, I was your assistant.

This story, though, has a happy ending.

About a dozen years ago, when I was a just-hired

young television writer and he was a just-arrived aspiring studio executive, his mom and my mom somehow met, and mothers being mothers, a couple of hours of my time was pledged to help the new kid figure out the town. Which I did, apparently. We had breakfast together, apparently. Advice was given, a bagel was toasted and buttered, and I, according to him, was nice and encouraging.

Lucky for me I was, because now the guy is a pretty successful and powerful studio executive, the maker of the very crucial funds disbursement decisions that I, as a writer and producer, like to be on the receiving end of. Which just goes to reinforce the only rule in Hollywood worth remembering: be nice to *everybody*. Because you never know.

The good news is the standard of good behavior in Hollywood is so low that to be known as a nice guy is really more a matter of *not* being known as a *not* nice guy.

I recently heard a story about a hot young producer and her assistant. Stuck on a story pitch, the producer decamped to a swank Las Vegas hotel, bringing along her assistant for some poolside brainstorming. As she floated, blissfully, in the hotel pool, her hapless assistant, clicking away on her laptop, sweltered in the desert sun. As the summer heat approached 105 degrees, the producer looked up at her sweat-drenched, fainting assistant and said, airily, 'You know, if you like, you can dangle your toes in the water. Just don't get the keyboard wet.'

There's a lot about the universe that's unknowable, of course, but there are three absolute certainties. One, there will come a time when that assistant, motivated by memories of heatstroke and a thirst for revenge, will have risen to a high and powerful post; two, there will come a time when that producer will be temporarily down on her luck and in need of a friend in high places; and three, the two will meet over a couple of bottles of water around a suede sofa. And by then it will be too late.

Be nice to *everybody*. Or at least, in Hollywood, don't be *not* nice to anybody. Because you never know.

And the truth is, success in Hollywood is often just a matter of hanging around here long enough and not taking 'no' for an answer. California has always attracted that kind of zealous operator. When you pick up the east side of the country and tilt things down to our way, what shakes loose are the kind of people who aren't very tethered to begin with. And those of us who have come here, to make it big in pictures, or grapes, or lettuce, or software, or real estate often forget that this nutty, loosely woven state has been a magnet for dreamers and no-accounts for a long time. Hollywood natives like to set themselves apart from the *arriviste* horde, but if you go back far enough – and sometimes, not really far back at all – every industry character shares a certain kind of seedy heritage with the earliest California Gold Rush newcomers. We all came, whether to pan for gold or to develop television sitcoms, to enjoy a dollop of prosperous counter-culture rootlessness. California's most exemplary

SET UP, JOKE, SET UP, JOKE

citizens, in other words, have had two things in common since 1849: blue jeans and greed.

We all came out to LA in waves, and those who came out at roughly the same time ended up knowing each other – like me and the now-studio-chief – and in some cases, became friends. It's like we were all part of the same freshman class, matriculates to the University of the Entertainment Industry, and so we either knew each other, from film school or threadbare parties or friend-of-a-friend-who's-an-assistant-to-somebody connections, or knew *of* each other.

I had a friend named Paul who came out to Hollywood a little bit after I did. We knew each other before – we went to the same high school – so when he came out, he gave me a call and we rekindled our friendship. He worked as a production assistant on a lot of movies and was often away on location. He and I would get together occasionally and drink beer and complain to each other about things that I'm sure were important then, but that have since slipped my mind. This was about six or seven years ago, and the things that concerned me around the time I turned thirty are vastly different from the things that concern me now, as I'm staring forty in the immediate distance.

One day, Paul called me up during a frantic production week and asked me out for a drink. He had been fired, he said. At the time, he was a young development executive at a busy and successful film production company. Getting fired from that kind of job was a rite of passage in a young executive's life, it seemed to me. We met that night, talked, drank a few beers, and said good night.

The next day, he shot himself.

This was my eulogy at his memorial service:

For Paul

The first time I saw Paul was 1981, or maybe 1982. We were in high school and Paul was my Cluster president. The school is divided into residential areas, clusters, and because it's a fancy boarding school and kids need things to put on their college applications, each cluster has a president. Paul was mine, which made sense, because Paul in high school was a lot like Paul later: charming, laughing, smiling. Same reassuring watery voice. If you were me in 1981 and you met Paul in 1981, you'd look up to him.

The last time I saw Paul was Monday, December 1st. He called me at work and asked if I was around later to get a beer. He was having a career crisis, he told me, and would fill me in later. We met at my house, walked to the Firehouse on Rose, had a few beers, and Paul told me that he had been fired. We talked for a long time about next steps, possibilities, things like that. We talked in that zig-zag fashion men use when they're circling around a big subject – switching from career and future to whether it would be fun to run a restaurant, to whether either one of us was going to go to our fifteenth high-school reunion. When you go to high school with someone, you've got a million and one things to talk about to keep you from talking about what's really important. We decided that we would both tell everyone we were going and pay the fee, but when the weekend came, we wouldn't show up. That way, we could avoid entreating phone calls from our Class Agent, not have to show up, and still get the T-shirt. They called Last Call, we finished our beers, walked back to my place, talked a bit more, then Paul drove home. A day later, he was dead.

The minute something like this happens, people tell you not to blame yourself. 'You couldn't know,' they say. 'People hide things.' A colleague of mine grabbed me a few minutes after I heard the news and said, in a low voice: 'This happened to me in 1967. Know this before you begin: you will never know why he did this.'

What did we talk about that night? Why didn't we get right into it? Why didn't he just tell me how hopeless and broken down he felt, how inconsolable. But if he had, what would I have done? What would I have said? Why didn't I tell him that night that he was a good friend to me – and he was: he would get me out of the house when I was going stir crazy, he would drag me to parties because he knew that if he didn't, I'd stay at home and play with the dog – are we flattering ourselves to think that if Paul had known, in those last awful lonely hours, how much the small things he did meant to us, that he wouldn't have done this? 'People hide things,' I know. Paul hid his sadness. But I hid my affection.

This terrible thing happened to Paul. But it also happened to us. He's not here to answer our questions, and if somehow he was, we still wouldn't understand. Paul was fighting a war against sadness. And he thought he was fighting it alone. How wrong he was.

A week after Paul's death, I wrote three letters to friends who have been good to me, who are important to me, but who I have never told. They were embarrassing letters to write, and the minute I dropped them in the mailbox, I regretted it. But they were sent.

I did these things in honor of Paul. My good friend Paul. A person I never knew.

It went over pretty well. The writer's ego in me is impossible to smother, so I was gratified when people came up to me later, after the service, to thank me for my words, and to ask for copies. But a true writer is more than an egomaniac. He's also a pathological liar. And in my eulogy, I hadn't told the truth.

'What did we talk about that night?' Well, actually, I remembered what we talked about that night. Paul asked me for a job. I told him that I couldn't give him one.

He didn't seem desperate to me – he asked me in an

offhand, joking, unserious way that I didn't know at the time – but have discovered since – is the tone some people use when they really are desperate, and not joking, and serious. So when he asked me, with a half-laugh and a shrug, I returned the favor. I pretended it was a joke, clapped him on the back and said something like, 'Hey man, anything I could get for you would be beneath you anyway.' And something empty like, 'This is an opportunity to be more entrepreneurial and independent, to strike out on your own, no one ever makes his mark in one of those small production boutiques, you hated it anyway, you were born for hands-on producing not idiotic office politics.' Or something.

And the truth is, I really couldn't have offered him a job anyway – though I was the executive producer of a – in the end, not very – successful half-hour television comedy, and in Paul's eyes seemed probably a lot more powerful than I was, or than I felt I was. Had the show been a hit, maybe I could have thrown my weight around and found something for him, anything. And then even if he went ahead and shot himself anyway, I wouldn't have felt like I felt when I heard the news two days later. Because what I felt then wasn't really surprise or shock, but a blast of recognition. *Oh*, I thought to myself, *that's what we were talking about. That's why the whole conversation felt so weird and awkward. That's why he said goodbye so formally. I knew something was different, I just didn't know what. And I didn't ask.* And then, *What kind of miserable shit am I, anyway?*

Because for me it was an act of indecency not to do what I could for my hurting friend, not to bend a few rules and stick my neck out. I failed the central and elemental test of friendship and loyalty. We had been in the same class, he and I – both literally and in the Hollywood sense – and I let him down.

What I should have said to Paul, when he was really down and, I found out later, suicidal, was 'Thanks for dragging me out to parties, and introducing me to pretty girls, and getting me out of the house, and not letting me talk to the same girl at the party all night and inviting me to have dinner with you and twenty-five of your awful, ghastly, chattering studio-executive friends, because, though I pretended to have a rotten time, I actually had a great time, and thanks.'

I mean, he probably would have shot himself anyway – I've read enough of the literature now to know that suicides aren't averted by friendly testimonials and do-nothing jobs – but at least he wouldn't have felt ... I don't know ... unimportant. Unappreciated. Unremembered. Whatever.

FADE OUT.

Meeting in an editing room, Thursday, 12:45 PM

'See? Right there! Right there!'

'What about it?'

'Can we just freeze for a moment on that frame?'

'Here?'

'Right. Right. See, this is sort of what we've been talking about during this process. I mean, it's a terrific act break, really. Just very strong and I think we get a sense of the guy, you know. What makes him tick and stuff. But something about it . . .'

'Do you not want to go to Paul's memorial service? Is it too heavy? I'm just trying to tell that part of the story with as much dignity as I can.'

'Oh, God, yeah, dignity. Of course. No, we think it's great, really. Just great.'

'Josh, can I chime in here?'

'Of course, Delia.'

'It's just that, one of the things we've been struggling with in this piece is the sense that people might feel that,

176

in a sense, that during the process you're describing – the story you're telling, there's a feeling of a sense that you may not be likable. That people may not like you very much. At all.'

'You guys have mentioned that, yeah.'

'So. . . . ?'

'But I thought you wanted it edgy. I mean, wasn't that the sense of the—'

'Yeah, yeah. No. Right. Yeah.'

'Yeah, no, right. Right.'

'Right, yeah, yeah. No. Right. Yeah.'

'So I guess what I was doing was trying to push it a bit. Even if that means I come off unlikable.'

'Not you, of course. I mean, your character. It's just that, when your friend asks you for a job—'

'Paul. His name is Paul.'

'Right. I mean, when Paul asks you for a job . . .'

'And you say . . . no . . .'

'It's just like all of a sudden, I'm thinking . . .'

'We don't like this guy very much.'

'Right, Josh. That was what I was trying to say. And then he commits suicide and we're sort of left with the feeling that . . .'

'Well, that you're responsible.'

'A little.'

'Well, more than a little.'

'Oh. So it comes off as my fault? Because I didn't give him a job?'

'A teeny skosh, yes.'

'I thought it was clear that I didn't really have a job to give him. And that, in the end, it wouldn't have made a difference.'

'I think what Josh is getting at is that for the purposes of the story, what if you did offer him a job?'

'So he wouldn't kill himself? Are you saying we should cut the whole section?'

'No, no, no, no. We really like that he kills himself.'

'We love that he kills himself.'

'Killing himself is great! Just great!'

'It's just that this way, you get to offer him a job like a good, likable person would, and he kills himself anyway, and you come off as a good guy.'

'What do you think of that? Remember, we're just tossing out ideas, here.'

'Well . . . I guess . . . I mean, what makes this difficult is that it really happened to me this way. And what I was going for – and I'm not saying it's successfully done, I'm just saying what I was going for – is some kind of telling of the story in a truthful way. I guess what I'm saying is that while I'd like to be more likable, I also have to be honest. At least when I'm telling this part of the story.'

'Well, no one wants you to change anything you don't feel comfortable changing.'

'This is your vision. Totally.'

'Totally.'

'Totally.'

'Keep it edgy!'

'Oh, yeah, right. Right. Yeah.'

'Yeah, no. No, keep it edgy, yeah.'

'Yeah. No.'

'Well, thanks.'

'Josh, can I chime in here a moment?'

'Sure, Delia.'

'What about the possibility that he offers Paul the job and Paul takes the job and then Paul doesn't commit suicide? Just a thought.'

'I like that a lot.'

'Me too.'

'Me too.'

'Me too.'

'And you know something? It really isn't all that much of a change.'

'Right, no, yeah, yeah, yeah, yeah, right, no, no.'

'Right, no, yeah, yeah, yeah, yeah, right, no, no.'

'Right, no, yeah, yeah, yeah, yeah, right, no, no.'

MAY: 'RERUN'

FADE IN:
INT. REGENCY HOTEL BAR – MANHATTAN
– NIGHT
I am sitting at the bar waiting to meet a friend. I know personally, or have worked with, or know people who have worked with, every single person in the bar.

I was here – right here, in this exact spot – one year ago tonight.

An agent slaps me on the back. His eyes are red and his tie is askew.

AGENT
   Hey man.
ME
   Hi.
AGENT
   Let me buy you a drink.
ME
   Thanks, but I'm on my way out.

AGENT

Then let me give you two tickets to the Hillary
Clinton thing.

ME

Gee, that's very generous of you. But, really,
I'm heading out.

AGENT

Hey, but, let me just say, dude, that it's awesome about your show, man. Awesome.
Awesome.

ME

Thanks. Really.

AGENT

Fuckin' great pilot. Totally great.

ME

Thanks. Really.

AGENT

So how many writers do you think you're
going to be hiring? Because we've got some
incredible guys who are just off deals, you
know . . .

ME

Not sure, really. Maybe when we get back to
LA we'll get into it.

AGENT

I'm telling you, it's a bloodbath out there.
I've got clients out of work, no deals, it's like
. . . it's like . . . and I'm here just workin' it
for them . . .

ME
> Yeah, hey, we're all in the same boat. Our
> deal is up in a month and . . .

AGENT
> You guys have a show on the air! It's fuckin'
> awesome! You're going to be fine!

ME
> Well, the ratings have to be good when we
> premiere, and . . .

AGENT
> Well, listen, I shouldn't be pitching my clients
> to you right now, when I'm so . . . so . . .

The agent begins staring at an attractive young woman who has just entered the bar.

ME
> So . . . wasted?

The agent moves off.

AGENT
> (to attractive woman)
> Would you like to meet Hillary Clinton?

CUT TO:
INT. HOTEL ELEVATOR – NIGHT
An executive from another studio steps into the elevator after me.

EXECUTIVE
> Hi!

ME
> Hi.

EXECUTIVE
  I'm off to see Hillary.
ME
  Great.
EXECUTIVE
  By the way, love the pilot, man. Just great.
  Congratulations. Gonna be a great series.
ME
  Thanks.
EXECUTIVE
  And I'm not just blowing smoke up your ass.
ME
  I appreciate your saying that.
EXECUTIVE
  I'm serious. If I had any money I'd be offering
  you a deal.
The elevator door opens. The executive steps out.
  EXECUTIVE (CONT'D)
  But I don't.
The doors close.
FADE OUT:

A market research testing facility in Burbank, California, Friday, 4:30 PM

'Okay, could everyone take their seats, please?'
  'How do these paddles work, dude?'
  'Okay, those are dials, and please take your seat, sir.'
  'I was told there would be pizza.'
  'Okay, pizza will be served – can we all sit down, please? – pizza will be served at the conclusion of the test screening.'
  'Are these the only seats?'
  'Can we all take a seat, please? And yes, ma'am, all the seats are the same. If you feel that you need a . . . more ample . . . size seat, perhaps we can find something . . .'
  'No, I can squeeze in.'
  'Wonderful.'
  'How do these paddle things go?'
  'Okay, those are dials and . . .'
  'Do the paddles, like, stick on to our chests or whatever for . . .'

'Okay, please, everyone, take a seat. No, the dials – they're dials, not paddles – are there for you to hold during the screening.'

'I don't have no paddles.'

'I got two paddles.'

'Okay, sir, please hand one of your dials – they're dials, not paddles – to the gentleman sitting next to you.'

'Mine's plugged in. Are the paddles supposed to be plugged in?'

'Yes, the dials – they're dials, not paddles – are each connected to a computer, which will record your reaction to the show we're about to screen.'

'Mine don't click or nothing.'

'I was told there would be pizza.'

'Mine don't work either.'

'My paddle is busted, dude.'

'Okay, the dials – they're dials, not paddles – don't click or anything. You just twist the knob to the right when you're enjoying the program, and then, if you find you're not enjoying it or are bored, just turn the knob back to the left.'

'I got a question.'

'Yes?'

'My paddle thingy isn't clicking.'

'Okay, the dials – they're dials, not paddles – don't click. They turn. To the right indicates that you're enjoying the screening. To the left indicates that you aren't. Your responses are sent to the computer through the wire attached to the handset, and the producers of the pro-

gram can get a sense of how much you as an audience have enjoyed their program. Okay? Are we ready to go?'

'I'm concerned about my privacy.'

'I'm concerned about the pizza.'

'Okay, pizza will be served after the screening. And your privacy is protected every step of the way, ma'am. No one in the testing facility has your name or address. If you still feel concerned about privacy, you may excuse yourself from this screening.'

'Do I still get the pizza?'

'No, ma'am.'

'I'll stay.'

'Okay, I think we're ready to begin the screening. Please, everyone, turn your dials to the center to begin. Make sure the red lines on the dial match the red line on the handset. Okay? Is everyone ready?'

'My paddles don't click.'

'Can we move the dial a little bit to the right if we're enjoying this part of the screening, too? I mean, if we're enjoying you?'

'Okay, the dials don't click – they're paddles, not dials – they turn. And we'd like everyone to center their dials so the red lines match up, okay? Okay, ready? Ready? Let's begin.'

SUMMER: 'KEEP IT SHUT'

FADE IN:
Television comedy isn't really 'written' in the traditional sense. It's quilted. The first draft of any episode, of course, has a single author. But after the first 'table reading,' which kicks off the production week, the script goes through several revisions. The entire writing staff gathers in one room, what has come to be called *The Room* in Industry parlance, and performs a collective rewrite. Whatever didn't work at that day's run-through is massaged and rewritten by a team of competitive, caustic comedy writers.

A full season's worth of episodes – about twenty-two in all – is an almost impossible task for one writer, or even two working as a team. Production itself requires so many other duties – casting, editing, listening to the network, working with actors, coming up with future episodes, rewriting scripts – that it's not realistic to write every episode yourself. So writers have to do something that is a real challenge for them: they have to work together politely. The protocol of *The Room* is as complicated and subtle as kabuki theater.

A rewrite session is like getting paid to undergo unpleasant group therapy. The writer sits in a room with the rest of the writers and someone called the 'writer's assistant' (who isn't a bottle of whiskey but is someone with lightning fast shorthand skills) and pitches new jokes as the group moves through the script. Every writer pretends to remember his first successful pitch, but it's unlikely to be the case. The whole thing is so nerve-shattering that your first week on a staff is spent sitting in cold sweaty clothes and seeing through a red fog. The rules are, as follows: 1. Never pitch a joke twice; if it doesn't get a laugh the first time, you lose. 2. Never pitch a problem in a script, especially a logic problem, something like 'Why wouldn't Sam just *call* Diane?' That's like pulling a loose thread in a cheap sweater, and you will be mercilessly abused by your colleagues for the rest of your career, which promises to be deadly and short. For to be branded 'bad in *the room*' around town is a sure way to get kicked out of the system.

A friend of mine told me that a certain legendary television writer/producer once dispensed this bit of wisdom, which for my money is the single best piece of advice I've ever heard: as my friend walked nervously into the room on his very first day in the television business, the old pro took him aside, and said to him in a gravelly murmur, 'Keep it shut.'

Once, to test his advice, I spent a week early in my career saying absolutely nothing in the room – just sitting quietly with a pleasant smile on my face. I was rewarded, on Friday afternoon, as I was walking to my car, with the current executive producer sidling up next to me, putting his arm around my shoulder, and saying, 'Great work this week. Really great.'

I'm not sure if he was kidding or not, and truth be told, it didn't really matter. What he meant was, I had been deemed 'good in the room.'

CUT TO:
INT. MY OFFICE – DAY
We are hiring writers for the staff of our new series. The phone rings continuously with agents pitching their clients to us. I am on the phone with a particularly aggressive one.

> AGENT (V.O.)
> Let me tell you, this guy is great. He's – and I'm running out of superlatives here – great. Great with story. Great with jokes.

> ME
> Fine. Send a script.

> AGENT (V.O.)
> Okay. Great.

> ME
> Thanks. 'Bye.

AGENT (V.O.)
One sec. There's just one thing you need to
know.
ME
What?
AGENT (V.O.)
He can't be in *The Room*.
ME
What?
AGENT (V.O.)
He can't be in the room. He just can't.
ME
Why?
AGENT (V.O.)
The last show he was on, they were very cruel.
There was a lot of . . . psychological . . . stuff
going on.
ME
Like what?
AGENT (V.O.)
Like some of the younger writers would
snigger at some of his joke pitches. Say things
like 'I think I saw that on an old *I Love Lucy*.'
When he didn't get one of their pitches, they'd
say it was a 'generational misunderstanding.'
During late rewrites, they kept ordering spicy
food that didn't agree with him. That sort of
thing.

ME

  Oh.

AGENT (V.O.)

  He's still a little shell-shocked. So instead of
  actually being in the room, he's at home on
  speakerphone.

ME

  He's home?

AGENT (V.O.)

  In his tub.

ME

  He's in the bath?

AGENT (V.O.)

  He finds the warm water very soothing.

ME

  Hmmmm.

AGENT (V.O.)

  Look, he's really been through the wringer.
  And let's be honest, you guys need some old
  timers on your staff.

ME

  How old is he?

AGENT (V.O.)

  Actually, federal law prohibits the asking of
  that question.

ME

  Sorry.

AGENT (V.O.)

  He's forty-two. But he thinks young.

CUT TO:

To be described, at forty-two years old, as a *young thinker*, is just one of the reasons that writers have it worse than actors.

Writers, though, in theory anyway, make their own breaks. To succeed as an actor, you need the right part and the right look. To succeed as a television writer, all you need to do is master the technology of the pencil. But success means working, anonymously, with other writers who probably hate you, or would if they knew how much you hate them. It means always trying to be funnier than the writer just below you in the hierarchy. It means that no matter how much everyone seems to get along, or how many times your bosses, the executive producers, tell you that you're doing a great job, you still take your career temperature every night on the way home. You still replay the day over and over in your head, asking yourself why you didn't think of the show-saving pitch, or the killer button to the last scene, and why the new kid, who looks twelve, did.

An actor friend of mine tells this story:

He is on an audition for a small part on a top-rated comedy series. He is, by way of background, a nice-looking guy and not untalented. He has, as we say around here, 'comedy chops,' which means, as we say around here, 'that he knows his way around a joke.' He can be funny, in other words. Halfway through his audition, while he is still speaking, the producer of the show turns to the casting director and says, in a loud voice, 'I told you to bring me some *good* looking people!'

The audition is over; my friend slinks out.

He told me this story over too many beers one night, and after listening to several hours of writers-get-no-respect and Hollywood-is-a-tough-place-for-a-writer from me. What could I do after hearing a story like that but mumble a few supportive comments and pick up the check?

Still, actors *ask* for that kind of abuse, and for all of their pretensions to 'the work' or 'the craft,' or, even more ludicrously, 'the art,' let's face it – it's still about 'everybody pay attention to me.' Writers, on the other hand, linger in the shadows and corrode quietly. I have seen actors waiting to audition for the same role genuinely wish each other well. 'Break a leg, man,' they'll say to each other, and you know they mean it because they're wearing that mentally-exhausted expression actors wear when they've said something unscripted.

Writers, of course, loathe each other. Writers, especially television writers (and even more especially, *bad* television writers) are enemies-list makers and gossip-spreaders, score-settlers and secret drinkers.

In fact, the only thing more bitter and furious than a roomful of writers is a convention hall full of writers, which unfortunately describes a meeting of the Writers Guild of America, West.

Every few years, the WGA – the putative screenwriters' trade union – suffers an institutional nervous breakdown as its members, made up entirely of writers and therefore unable to agree on anything, attempts to agree on the terms of a new contract with the studios.

The sticking point invariably centers at some new profit source exploited by the studios – DVD sales, say, or pay-per-view satellite broadcasts – that they have neglected to pass on to the writer. The working writers – and that number is somewhat smaller than 100 per cent of the membership of the WGA West – tend to be philosophical about these issues. Sure, we get angry and bitter. But we're writers. We were angry and bitter *before* we got into this business. In some cases I could mention, anger and bitterness were the primary inspiration for a particular writer to saddle up and move to Los Angeles. I know one guy who became a television writer simply because it afforded him the opportunity to write on a cop show and name all the strippers, whores, and girl junkies after his mother.

The non-working writers are a more querulous lot. Freed from the burden of actually having to show up to a job every day, they look to the occasional WGA strike to round out their social calendar, to catch up with old friends on the picket line. And since all writers crave excuses for not writing, what better excuse for being unproductive than a strike. Writing? Not me. I'm *honoring my brother and sister scribes!* I'm *taking part in the labor movement!* Lazy? Untalented? Nope. Just committed to social justice. Rarely has sitting on your ass outside the studio gates, carrying a picket sign while eating a ham sandwich ever seemed so glamorous.

So the working writers – especially the young ones –

hate strike talk. And the non-working writers see a strike as a great way to get out of the house. The remaining group – the rich writers who are not working by choice – form a kind of swing vote. They all meet at the WGA Membership meeting, an event so chaotic and anger-charged that it's hard to believe it's taking place in Southern California. It seems almost Bosnian in the intensity of its bitterness.

CUT TO:
INT. SANTA MONICA CONVENTION
CENTER – NIGHT
I am milling around the lobby of the convention center, waiting to get a cup of coffee. Behind me, in the auditorium, I can hear the speaker, a WGA board member, in mid-reminiscence.

> BOARD MEMBER (O.S.)
> . . . and it was here, in this convention center,
> that I was privileged, in nineteen hundred and
> seventy-two, to hear the very moving words
> of Krisnamurti Singthongpet, a very wise man
> who was instrumental in getting my then-
> wife to agree to an 'open marriage,' which,
> at the time . . .

I move a few writers closer to the coffee urn. I see an acquaintance of mine, a man I know for a fact to be worth serious coin – in the tens of millions of dollars – stuff sugar packets into his jacket pockets.

Back in the auditorium, I hear the meeting get underway.

A member is using his 'free speech' time to rail against the perpetual WGA meeting topic, the Hollywood Blacklist of the 1950s. The Blacklist was, essentially, a list of writers who, because of their affiliation with the Communist Party, were unemployable by the major studios. It now functions as a handy excuse for older writers who, because of their incredible lack of talent, were unemployable by the major studios.

ELDERLY VOICE (O.S.)
(shouting every few words)
... and I am SO ANGRY! The blacklist DESTROYED this town! It RAPED this industry! And it IMPOVERISHED our culture! I was CHEATED out of credit for pictures that I WROTE! I never saw my OWN goddam NAME on ANY of my BEST work. *The Cannibal Fixers* – NO CREDIT! *Bongo Beauties* – NO CREDIT!

I move two science fiction writers and one children's cartoon writer closer to the coffee. An older writer sidles up next to me.

OLDER WRITER
Hey. I know you.

ME
Hi.

OLDER WRITER
You spoke on a panel discussion I went to.

ME
Hi.

OLDER WRITER
So, do you ever hire older writers on those
TV shows of yours?

This is an inevitable question, and a touchy one. Older
writers often feel pushed aside by younger ones, and resent
the richer deals of today's business. 'Ageism' is what they
call it, with a writer's tin ear for self-irony.

ME
Oh, by all means. We like to work with writers
who have more experience. In fact, we work
regularly with two or three writers in their
sixties.

I mention their names. The older writer shrugs.

OLDER WRITER
Oh, those guys. I know those guys. They're
good writers. But I don't mean them. I mean,
do you ever hire just *ordinary* older writers?

CUT TO:

The great benefit of the Writers Guild of America, West
is its rich and full health plan. Everything is covered,
including thirty days every five years at the Betty Ford
Clinic, which seems generous to the point of encour-
agement. In a town like this one, filled with vegetarians,
exercise addicts, healthy livers, and hypochondriacs –
and these groups intersect in a big way – handing someone
a medical care blank check is like handing someone a
hobby.

And let's face it: the bulk of the WGA membership is

made up of hard-working, fairly successful retired writers who are looking for something to do. I'd rather they spend their days at the gastroenterologist than walking the picket line.

Years ago, a few months after landing my first writing job in Hollywood, the membership of the WGA was seriously considering a strike. After a long, screaming membership meeting (try to imagine a dysfunctional family of 300 sitting down to Christmas dinner and you'll get the picture) they – we, I should say – decided, in true writers' form, to postpone any decision for a month or two.

I walked out to my car with another writer, about twenty years my senior.

'I'm worried about a strike,' I said.

'A strike is what we need around here,' he muttered bitterly.

'But I'll be broke in a month. I need to work,' I said.

'You'll be better off in the long run,' the older writer replied, patting me reassuringly on the shoulder. 'Did I ever tell you about how we won the thirty days in Betty Ford? We did it by walking out! By sticking together!'

'But don't you think the studios have a point?' I asked. 'After all, they take all the risk.'

'To hell with them!' he shouted. 'Fuck management! Fuck the power structure! Fuck those fucking fuckers!'

And with that, he sped off in his BMW 750il.

The Betty Ford Center treats many addictions, though not, thankfully, the addictions to inappropriate rage and luxury automobiles. It leaves these uncured, giving the Hollywood writer a reason to get out of bed.

A few years ago, a network television executive was asked to describe his ideal audience. He was looking for 'voracious consumers of free television,' he said, people who couldn't afford cable services, didn't have jobs during the day or reasons to go to bed early, and who were easily overwhelmed by programming choices and so preferred to stick with one channel throughout the day.

His ideal audience, in other words, was the very young, the very old, and the very sick.

Today, the target audience has shifted a bit. The very old and the very sick are on their own. The desirable demographics that all the major networks battle over are the very young, the somewhat young, and the under-thirty. That's the main reason network television has an eerie *Lord of the Flies* vibe to it: almost every show features, exclusively, characters without a trace of the tiny lines and wrinkles that begin to appear around, say, the age of thirty-two.

Television advertisers want young audiences, it seems, so programs that skew young command higher advertising rates. The theory goes something like this: old people read magazines and newspapers, they watch the news channels and listen to the radio – that makes finding them a lot easier and therefore cheaper. Young people, on the other hand, spend a great deal of time listening to depressing music and doing alarming things to their hair, not reading magazines and definitely not bothering with the newspaper, so when you get one trapped in front of a television set, grab him. Their feckless indolence makes them worth more, perversely. The poor over-forty set, with their good jobs and sense of civic responsibility, are a dime a dozen.

Perhaps more importantly, old people – again, I'm using the Standard Industry Definition of *old people*, which is anyone over forty – have already decided so many things about their lives – what foods they like to eat, which soft drinks they prefer, how they like to cure their headaches and their stuffy noses, things like that. Young people – untrustworthy, promiscuous, persuadable – tend not to have settled on a few key brands, and can thus be persuaded that doctors have indeed recently created an ointment that makes pimples disappear, that switching soft drink preferences increases opportunities for casual sex, and that certain fast-food restaurants are merry places filled with attractive, laughing young people.

A few years ago, we produced a series in which the two main characters, in an act of purely contrarian bloody-mindedness, were in their sixties. In other words, the combined age of our two lead actors was roughly that of all six *Friends* combined. Our audience was respectably large, but unrespectably old. The people who watched our show all had jobs and mortgages and expenses – in other words, useless scum.

'Hey, you guys were cancelled?' People older than forty

would ask that question, and I always dreaded giving the answer. 'But why?' they would ask. 'I *loved* that show.'

And I would say, 'Well, the audience demographic wasn't in the desirable range for network television.'

And they would look confused.

And then I would be forced to say that while we had a great many viewers, their average age was forty-plus, which made them unimportant to advertisers and, consequently, to network executives. And then the color would drain out of the face of the person I was talking to, and he would stammer and cough in the half-rage half-sadness appropriate to someone who has just been told that his *entire life*, its needs, triumphs, accomplishments, and meaning, is *undesirable*, and that America's vast army of consumer product manufacturers and advertisers wouldn't care if he and his contemporaries dropped dead on the spot. Eventually, his eyes would dilate and fix themselves on the middle distance.

And I'd be glad to still be in my thirties. Barely.

CUT TO:

I am out having a beer with my plastic surgeon friend. He has a booming Beverly Hills practice and always has great stories, mostly about liposuction and breast augmentation. Most of his patients are involved in the entertainment industry, and come to him for simple nips and tucks here and there – to be, what he calls, 'refreshed.' He is talking about one of his new patients, a well-known young actress. He won't tell me her name.

'She is absolutely beautiful,' he says. 'She has a *perfect* body.'

'Who is it?' I want to know.

He shakes his head. 'Can't say. Patient confidentiality.'

'What does she want done?'

'Her neck,' he answers. 'Every other part of her is perfect.'

'Her *neck*? What was wrong with her neck?'

'Nothing, really. A little loose. Some diminished tautness. Nothing major,' he says. 'But the neck is tricky. You can't really wait until it sags and completely loses its elasticity. You have to adjust it a little bit every year or so. Take it in an inch now and then. You can't put the neck off, like the chin or the forehead. Gotta start early.'

'How old is she?'

'That's the problem. She's twenty-eight. She waited *way* too long. Should've come to me four years ago.'

I laugh and shake my head. To be twenty-eight and worried about your neck! I take a sip of my beer and look at my reflection in the mirror at the back of the bar. I think I look okay. Not great, but okay. I lift my chin and tilt my head back to get a good look at my neck. My friend watches me do this.

He clears his throat. 'You know,' he says, 'you'd be surprised how many of my patients are men. It's considered totally acceptable for a guy to want to get a little work done.'

I scoff.

'I'm serious,' he says. He mentions the name of a young actor in a hugely-popular sitcom. 'He came to me for a simple nose job, and left with a chin implant, an ear bob, and a male breast aug.'

'You gave him breasts?' I ask, laughing.

'I gave him *pectorals*,' he says. 'I turned him into a romantic lead. Before me, he was strictly character roles.'

'Forget it,' I say. 'I'm not an actor and I'm not paying you $25,000 to stretch my neck.'

'Don't flatter yourself. The neck is the least of your problems. For you, I'd recommend an eye tuck, a forehead lift, a chin implant, a jaw shape, and some lipo around the jowls *before* we even think about the neck.'

'Forget it,' I say. 'I'm going to let myself deteriorate naturally.'

'Try this,' he says.

He puts my hands together, as if in prayer. He tucks my thumbs under my chin, and places my two index fingers against my nose.

'Now,' he says, 'leaving your thumbs touching, open your hands up, like you're trying to smooth out your face. Pull back gently.'

I do it.

'Now, hold,' he says. 'And look in the mirror.'

I do. I see a tight, wrinkle-free face. I see a pronounced jawline. I see the familiar facelift perpetual smile. I see myself, refreshed.

'Forget it,' I say, still holding back my face.

'Suit yourself,' he says, finishing the rest of his beer.

I drop my face and do the same. We pay for our drinks and walk to our cars.

'Tonight,' he says, ominously, 'you'll brush your teeth and look at yourself in the mirror, and you'll think, "hey, I don't look bad." And later this week, maybe in the morning after you've shaved, you'll chuckle to yourself and do the thumbs-under-the-chin trick, just for a laugh. But you'll start to notice all the little droops and sags. The folds of skin that suddenly appear. The creases where nothing should crease. And then maybe you'll hear about a couple of young writers, guys in their early twenties, who are suddenly hot. And the years will start running together in your memory and teenaged boys will start calling you "sir" and the grey hairs will start sprouting and every single morning you'll tuck your thumbs under your chin, "just to see," you'll tell yourself. And then one day you'll be in my office.'

I stare into the night, car keys still dangling in my hand.

'Who are you?' I ask. 'The devil?'

My friend laughs. 'Nope. Just a plastic surgeon in Beverly Hills.'

He gets into his new Mercedes and speeds away. How many 'breast augs' does it take to buy that car? How many chin lifts for the Chevy Blazer, his other car? How many 'refreshers' for the two weeks in Vail, Colorado? I'll let myself turn into a raisin before I'll give him one penny, I think to myself. Nobody is retiring on *my* neck.

But then I remembered:

A year or two ago, during a casting session, I ran into

a former high-school classmate. I had just stepped out to refill my coffee, and there she was: still ravishing, sitting with a dozen or so other actresses, ready to audition for me, my producing partner, and our casting staff.

'Hey!' I shouted.

'Hey!' she shouted back.

We gave each other a little squeeze and a peck on the cheek. I remembered her as a beautiful girl, and here she was, in my office, a beautiful woman.

'How long has it been?' I asked, and as I started to mentally calculate the intervening years, I felt her hand close tightly around my wrist.

'Do you have a sec?' she asked.

I walked with her to the coffee machine. She whispered frantically. 'See, I play twenty-three, twenty-four, okay?'

'Excuse me?'

'I'm twenty-four. Twenty-five at the max.'

'But we were in the same high-school class,' I said, still not getting it. She looked at me for a moment, eyes wide and fierce, like she was trying to drill her meaning into my head.

'Oh,' I said, finally getting it. '*Oh*.'

'It's just, you know, the *business*,' she said.

'Should I pretend not to know you?'

She put her hand on my shoulder and shook her head in pity.

'No,' she said, 'you can say you know me. But I'd appreciate it if you said that you were *better* friends with my *older* sister.'

I didn't even have time to spin some filthy casting-couch fantasies. I was shunted off into an undesirable demographic. I'm too old, even for people my own age.

CUT TO:

INT. MY CAR – DAY

I'm on the phone. An agent is pitching another client.

> ME
>
> Sorry, we're all staffed up.
>
> AGENT (V.O.)
>
> Really?
>
> ME
>
> Really.
>
> AGENT (V.O.)
>
> No, really?
>
> ME
>
> Yes, really.
>
> AGENT (V.O.)
>
> So who did you hire?
>
> ME
>
> Well, I'd rather not say right now. We're still
> waiting to close a few deals.
>
> AGENT (V.O.)
>
> Oh, okay. I understand. So who did you hire?
>
> ME
>
> I can't say. We're waiting to close a few
> deals.
>
> AGENT (V.O.)
>
> Yeah, but can I just know?

ME
No.
AGENT (V.O.)
C'mon. They think I'm too old over here at
the agency. They're sending out signals around
here that they're thinking about firing me, and
it'll really help if I had some titbit to show
how plugged in and on top of things I am.
ME
What kind of signals?
AGENT (V.O.)
Things like, one of the younger partners took
me aside Monday morning and said, 'We're
thinking about firing you.' And then one of
the twenty-something assistants mentioned
casually that everyone here hates me. Subtle
stuff.

CUT TO:
One of the pleasures of having a television show in production is hanging out with the other writers on the staff
while eating junk food, gossiping, telling filthy jokes, and
complaining. Writers, in general, tend to do these things
anyway – at any lunch spot in Hollywood, at any time,
there will almost always be a table of writers where the
phrases 'stingy rat bastards' and 'smug network eunuch
punks' can be overheard – but somehow it means more
when all of the writers are complaining about the same
person while working on the same show.

The other pleasure is sharing particularly egregious agent stories.

When our pilot was ordered for the fall schedule, we hired a small staff of very talented writers, with varying degrees of television writing experience. The least experienced writer, it turns out, was a real find: funny, polite, literate, and saddled with enough personal eccentricities to make talking behind his back interesting. He was good enough at his job, in fact, to have stirred our sympathies (first-time staff writers make very little money) so we raised his salary a pinch.

In Hollywood, of course, you don't just call the hireling into your office and bark at him, gruff-but-lovable-style: 'Hey, shitbird, you're doin' a great job. The pay packet's going to be heavier from here on out.' Instead, you must telephone a reedy-voiced bureaucrat who works at the studio in a department called, with ominous vagueness, 'Business Affairs,' tell that person to call the writer's agent, have the writer's agent call the writer, and then, after the agent has called the writer with the news, drag the writer in your office before he can blurt out 'Thanks for the raise!' in front of the other writers on the staff who didn't get a raise and aren't getting a raise until their contracts specifically call for it, because, after all, you're not made of money, are you?

Here's what happened: the staff writer was at home, writing a draft. We placed a call to Business Affairs, and kicked off the dominoes. The next day the writer sauntered into work, full of praise for his agent, who, we were informed, had called the writer the day before to tell him that after some 'secret negotiations' and 'major arm-twisting,' the agent had wrangled some extra money for the fledgling writer – 'We've sweetened the pot for you, kiddo,' the agent told the client, 'We went to the wall for you, and guess what? They blinked.'

CUT TO:
INT. HAVANA ROOM – DAY
A swank Hollywood cigar club. I am having lunch with an agent who is a partner in the agency that represents me. I have just told him the preceding story.

> AGENT
> Are you kidding me?
>
> ME
> Nope. Happened just like that.
>
> AGENT
> I think that's . . . that's . . . *immoral*. And I'm an agent.

I laugh.

> AGENT (CONT'D)
> He cheated his client out of knowing that he was doing a good job. What a creep. The kid should dump that agent.
>
> ME
> I agree.
>
> AGENT
> So did you set the kid straight?
>
> ME
> You bet.

AGENT

Good. You know, the business, it's getting so sick. So cutthroat. Used to be, you wouldn't lie to a client and you wouldn't hit on someone else's client.

ME

'Hit on?'

AGENT

Yeah. Try to steal. You know, 'hit on,' 'flirt with,' 'seduce.'

ME

Interesting terminology.

AGENT

If someone else's client *called you first*, then you could go to bed with him. But only if the guy called *you*.

ME

'Go to bed with?'

AGENT

Sign as a client.

The agent waves to a few men in suits at another table.

AGENT (CONT'D)

Look at this place. Filled with agents. It's a real pick-up place. You must get 'hit on' a lot.

ME

Well, yes.

AGENT

But you're happy with your representation, right?

ME
    Yes, of course.
AGENT
    (shrugging)
    If you weren't, you'd tell me.
A long pause.
    AGENT (CONT'D)
    Right?

CUT TO:
INT. SOUNDSTAGE – NIGHT
We're shooting an episode of our series. As the cameras reload, the audience warm-up guy goes into his act. I'm standing on the stage floor. A young agent at the agency that represents me approaches.
    YOUNG AGENT
    Hey, man. How's it goin'?
All young agents speak fluent 'guy.'
    ME
    Fine. You?
    YOUNG AGENT
    Cool.
Because I don't speak fluent 'guy,' the conversation falters. A long pause.
    YOUNG AGENT (CONT'D)
    Heard about what that dude did to that dude
    you have on staff. That is totally messed up,
    man.

ME
>Yes, I agree.

YOUNG AGENT
>(surveying the knot of writers hovering nearby)
>So which one is he?

I point him out.

YOUNG AGENT (CONT'D)
>'Scuse me.

He canters over to the writer.

DISSOLVE TO:

EXT. STUDIO PARKING LOT – LATER THAT NIGHT

We've wrapped. Another show in the can. I walk to my car. At the far end of the parking lot, through the gauzy evening mist, I can make out the twin silhouettes of the young agent and the staff writer.

The writer is standing by his open car door. The agent is leaning against it, talking with animated intensity. The writer is being 'hit on.'

It's like a Hopper painting: lonely, sad, funny, and a perfect snapshot of Hollywood. One guy wants to make a sale; the other guy just wants to go home.

CUT TO:

In the end, the writer left his agent for the young agent in the parking lot. It was a principled decision, of course – no one likes being lied to – but it was also an emotional

one – everyone likes being hit on. To be worth a seduc-
tion scene (something along the lines of 'you're so talented' and 'you've got a huge future') just makes it sweeter.
The truth, though, is that I have an ironclad contract
with the writer which gives me an option on his services
for three years. So whoever he signs with – the old agent,
the new agent, his mother, his priest – he's mine for three
seasons at a previously agreed-upon price. He's young.
He'll figure it out.

A writer friend of mine tells this story:

He is working on a television series with a predomi-
nantly black cast. It is early in the run of the series –
early enough, in fact, for most of the cast to be driving
the cars they drove before winning the part. (There is no
sight more soothing to a writer than the sight of an actor
driving a Subaru.)

The episode that they are rehearsing that week is a
simple one: two of the male characters are supposed to
take care of a third character's apartment. It is filled with
expensive and fragile trinkets. Connect the dots: hijinks
ensue.

The block comedy scene – industry lingo for the big
scene in the second act when the hilarity kicks in – is a
simple affair of two clumsy men, a bunch of breakable
props, and a small fire.

After a decent run-through, one of the actors knocks
on my friend's office door. He is angry. He launches into
a speech. His voice is trembling with anger: he is humiliated by the script; he refuses to perform it again; it is a

racist and vile depiction of his people, reinforcing the clumsy, slow-witted, trip-over-your-own-feet stereotype of yesteryear, and as a proud African-American male he will not demean himself or denigrate his race in such a grotesque manner.

My friend takes a deep breath. He nods sympathetically and shrugs. 'Consider it gone,' he says quietly. 'Though it's a shame. You really are a master of physical comedy.'

A long pause.

'I am?'

'Are you kidding? You're telling me you haven't had training?'

'Well, nothing formal.'

'What can I say? It's . . . Chaplinesque. But forget it. It's cut.'

Another long pause.

In the end, they did the scene as written. Flattery always, always, *always* works.

CUT TO:

INT. MY OFFICE – DAY

We have filmed the first few episodes of our series. Things are going well, so we go through the day uneasily. Every day without a disaster just makes the inevitable one that much more brutal. And the inevitable one takes place a week from now, when we have our broadcast premiere. Which means we'll get our first set of ratings.

It's a strange sort of lag, but familiar, too. We're deeply into the production process – characters have been defined, and in some cases redefined; story areas have been dis-covered and tossed out; the creaky ensemble of strangers has begun to click together. The show, in other words, is working.

Except that nobody has seen it yet. *We* think we're doing fine. *We* love the show. America, though, has yet to be consulted. And when that happens, when we have our opening night, all of the enthusiasm and humming energy and optimistic window-shopping will either seem brilliantly intuitive or hilariously delusional.

It's this way all over Hollywood. It takes a year, at least, for an actor's hard work, or a director's vision, to make it to a screen near you – and by that time, they've probably forgotten the tantrums and struggles and the certain knowl-edge that the picture they're working on is *just absolute crap*. Maybe, in the ensuing months, their memories have embroidered the experience into something good and aus-picious. So later, when the movie comes out, and they're pushing it at press junkets worldwide, they have to relive the entire episode, and are humiliated a second time; and later still, when it comes out on DVD and there's another round of humiliations. And on. And on. The lag is a killer.

In television, if possible, it's worse. Because you're always about eight or ten episodes ahead of your air date, in the early stages you really have the sense that the show is getting better all the time. It's a foolish sense, though, because the audience is going to see them *in order*, bad ones first. And they may not stick around to watch a series get better.

Today, though, the universal symbol of series success has come over the transom in the form of a 'spec,' or sample, script. In order to get a job writing for television, you must first complete a few sample scripts of some of the better shows on the air. The logic, I guess, is that if you can write a good episode of *Frasier*, then you'll be able to master the writing chores on the show about the zany family and their robot housekeeper.

You only write specs for shows that have an air of longevity. So it's with some excitement that I announce to my partner that some aspiring writer has penned his own script for our little show, and although studio policy, good sense, and much better things to do argue against it, I open the envelope and dig in. Oh, sure, there's a tiny voice in my head saying *Hey, wait a minute – the show hasn't even aired yet. Who could possibly have seen it? How did anyone know enough about it to write a spec episode?* But I hate that voice. It's an irritating voice. I prefer the voice that says *Wow, this is like some kind of sign from the heavens. The buzz must be great around this show! It's going to be a hit; no, wait, it IS a hit; no, wait, it's a MONSTER hit. It's the seventh arrondissement, right? That's the really good one? Rue du Bac? Rue Jacob? Right? Right?*

CUT TO:
INSERT SHOT: THE COVER PAGE OF THE SPEC
The title of the episode is 'Joey Moves In,' which I find odd. There is, to my knowledge, no 'Joey' character on

my series. I try to keep up on these things. But the name rings a faint bell.
INSERT SHOT: FLIPPING PAGES
Huge speeches for 'Joey.' Pages and pages of 'Joey' dialogue. 'Joey' this and 'Joey' that.

CUT TO:
Joey, it turns out, is technically a character on our series. He had one line, in episode two. He was a customer in a bookstore. The spec entitled, with alarming stupidity, 'Joey Moves In,' was penned by the actor who played the part. He has taken the bull by the horns. He has written himself a role as a series regular. He thinks, like most actors, that most writers are mildly mentally retarded and will not notice that the 'Joey' actor and the 'Joey Moves In' author are one and the same. Worse, he thinks I will finish his script. I don't.

Actors have a difficult life out here, of course. Many of the talented ones never make it. Some simply aren't lucky. And others, the really talented ones, aren't good-looking enough.

The actor who essayed the role of 'Joey,' (one tiny line: 'Did you like this book, man?') was handsome enough, and will probably eke out some sort of living. But like most actors in his position, he couldn't quite master the requirements of the role of 'Joey,' which were, simply, to say his line in as neutral a tone as possible, and then to move quickly away. The first day of rehearsal he did it perfectly and we laughed, because, after all, we wrote it. The second day of rehearsal, emboldened by his triumph, 'Joey' put a little more spin on the ball and blew it. The third day, he really loaded up the attitude ('*Hey*, did you enjoy *this* book, man?!') and it was time to have a little talk with him. 'Hey, man,' I said to him after the run-through, in my best actor-dude dialect, 'throw it away, okay?'

He looked at me blankly.

'Throw it away,' I said. 'Just say it. Just say the line straight.'

'Really?' he asked.

'Really,' I answered.

'But I'm trying to activate my choice.'

I looked at him blankly.

He clarified: 'I'm trying to give Joey a little texture.'

'Well, don't,' I said. 'Just throw it away.'

When we shot the episode two days later, he was a lot better. But still never as good as he was that first day, before he started acting.

CUT TO:

INT. MY OFFICE – DAY

I am on the phone with my agent, and I mention the spec script and the day player.

>   ME
>   (winding up)
>   And that just proves what I've always said.
>   Actors are crazy. Completely out of touch
>   with reality. Easy to flatter, easy to manipu-
>   late, impossible to treat as equals.

218

MY AGENT (V.O.)
(laughing)
I just had this exact conversation! I was just
talking to the guy who runs your studio and
he said the exact same thing to me, in the
exact same words! Isn't that weird?
ME
That is odd. Which actor was he talking
about?
MY AGENT (V.O.)
Oh, he wasn't talking about actors. He was
talking about *writers*.
ME
Oh.

CUT TO:

When a writer gives you his script to read, he usually
says something totally dishonest like, 'Hey, let me know
what you *really* think, okay?' In other words, he wants
you to be honest. He can take it, he says. 'I know there're
some rough spots in the second act,' he may say, 'so just
give me your honest opinion.'

There is, though, only one response that he will find
acceptable. He wants you to read his script in a kind of
rapture, laughing yourself in tears at the right spots, emit-
ting low moans of pleasure or surprise here and there, until
you finally wipe the mist from your eyes, hold the script
to your breast, look at him with awe and gratitude and a
dash of what-a-terrible-burden-such-insight-must-be pity,

and say in a low, quavery voice, 'This is one of the greatest scripts I have ever read. It is absolutely perfect.'

Anything short of that – anything even a *fraction* short of that – will be a crushing disappointment. The writer will say something like, 'You hate it, don't you?' And you will say something like, 'No, no! I love it! But you're right about the second act. But I love it!'

The writer will respond with: 'You hate the second act? I thought that was the best part.'

And you will counter with: 'I *like* the second act. But it's just a little slow.'

Writer: 'Why are you trying to destroy me?'

You: 'I'm just being constructive.'

Writer: 'You call *that* constructive?'

You: 'What do you want me to say? That it was one of the greatest scripts I have ever read? That it's absolutely perfect?'

Writer: 'Yes!'

You: 'I thought you wanted my honest opinion.'

Writer: 'I want *that* to *be* your honest opinion.'

Which is why so many writers have been married so many times.

Having a show in production is like being in a continuous note session. Story ideas, scripts, run-throughs, rough-cuts – all of these phases require the input of the network and the studio. Mostly, these notes follow a simple pattern: everyone will read the script, digest it, identify the one or two things about it which make it unique, and then ask us to remove those one or two things. Really talented executives know all the traps of giving a writer notes, so almost every note session begins with, 'This is the best script I have ever read. It is absolutely perfect.'

Followed by: 'But we have a few notes.'

Knowing how to make enormous changes sound like tiny 'adjustments' is, in fact, the only useful skill most studio types possess.

'Is there any way,' we were once asked by a studio executive, 'that you could show the main character *doing* something incredibly heroic and totally *saving* the day in a simple one-page scene we can slap on the top?'

We shook our heads.

'C'mon, guys,' the exec said, 'a simple one-pager. Boom, he does something heroic, everybody loves the guy, boom, back into the story.'

Hollywood is a collaborative place. Everyone has to work together in some kind of harmony, after all, with mutual respect and good manners intact for the next project – which is why, by the way, so many of those projects are so awful – so *getting* notes takes as much elaborate courtesy as *giving* them.

'Good idea,' we usually say after hearing a particularly asinine suggestion, 'we'll take a look at that.'

And we assiduously write down every idea, no matter how foolish or nutty or destructive.

Another trick we use is to lavish praise on the most innocuous note – can the main character have a dog, say, or can his bicycle be bright red? – something easy to change and totally irrelevant, which enables us to ignore several other stupid suggestions that *aren't* irrelevant and would *hurt* the script while still seeming like 'team players.'

Once, in a meeting with the studio, after they had just finished giving notes, the executive added, in a smooth manage-the-talent tone, 'Great script, guys.'

But I was unable to let him think he's managing me. I had to manage *him*.

'Great notes,' I replied.

He looked at me uneasily.

'Really?' he asked. 'You writers usually hate getting notes from the studio.'

'No, no,' I said. 'Well, not from *you*. Yours are particularly good.'

'Well, thank you.'

'Especially the one about the red bicycle. I think that will clarify the core conflict in that character's arc,' I blathered.

'You're full of shit,' he said. 'Now, please, just listen to the notes and see if you can't implement them without screwing up your . . . what do you writers call it? . . . your *vision*. Stop trying to manage me.'

I looked up from my paper, where I have been assiduously copying down everything he says.

'Good idea,' I said. 'We'll take a look at that.'

Back when I was an unemployed film student, I convinced myself that spending all day at the movies wasn't a sign of laziness, but of a deep commitment to my craft and an equally strong interest in what I pretty unironically called *the language of cinema*.

It also cost about eight dollars a day, at which point I realized that it was either *the language of cinema* or *the consumption of beer*, and, well, figure it out yourself.

The good news for anyone who wants to watch their movie and drink it too, however, is that at any given time in Hollywood, someone is holding a test screening of his most recent film. Sometimes these are held in large theaters – easy to slip into anonymously – and sometimes in plush, rented screening rooms with free snacks galore. And because the guest lists for these things are drawn up and supervised by the lowest ranking person around – the press assistant's assistant, the studio boss's water boy, the guy who underlines *Variety* for his boss the talent agent – it's easy to crash any screening with just a simple phone call.

Hollywood is a vast, rainless version of *Upstairs, Downstairs* – all the downstairs types know each other, hang out together, exchange gossip, and call each other on their bosses' cell phones. It's a class system organized by age: people in their early twenties tend to know everyone else in town that age, and the result is an invisible web that links the assistants, the young actors, the agents-in-training, and, lucky for me, the unemployed film students.

A free screening brings out the web in force. One assistant calls another, and before you know it, dozens of unemployed young lazybones are parking their rusted

Subarus and smoking Hondas on side streets all over town (valet parking is five dollars, you see), donning their very best leather jackets, and heading into the VIP line.

After the screening, we'd walk out into the lobby, past the phalanx of studio executives and marketing gurus, past the actors and their cigarettes, and finally, past the nervous-looking director. I'd always make eye contact with the director, smile knowingly, then give him a thumbs-up sign, like I was a big shot who knew what was what, like I was an *important person* and not *an unemployed film student driving a Subaru.*

Once, sauntering out, I gave the half-smile/thumbs-up to the director – a particularly famous and powerful one this time – and was almost out the door when he called me back.

'Hey!' he shouted.

I stopped. Turned around. My stomach kept turning.

'Yeah?' I said, trying to act cool.

'Whadja think?' he asked, mistaking me for an *important person.*

I shrugged nonchalantly, though inside my leather jacket, I was drenched in sweat.

'Could lose twelve minutes, easy.'

The director looked at me for a moment. Then nodded.

'Yeah,' he said. 'Faster is better.'

He started to say something else, but I didn't hear him. I was dashing out to my Subaru.

Last month, I was invited to a screening of a major picture with a November release date. The guy who invited me is the president of production at a large movie studio in town, though I remember him as the guy who used to underline *Variety* for his talent-agent boss back when I was an unemployed film student. This proves that if you stick around Hollywood long enough, good things happen.

The movie, though, was not a good thing. It was an awful thing. An awfully long thing.

Walking out of the screening – held in a plush, intimate screening room with free drinks and snacks, the kind of place where I used to eat enough for dinner and take enough for lunch the next day – my friend pulled me aside.

'What did you think?' he asked, worried.

I shrugged. 'It's not bad,' I lied. 'How close is it to being done?'

'How *close*?' he hollered in a whisper. 'That's our final cut. That's it.'

'Oh,' I said.

'So what do you think?'

I shrugged again. 'To tell you the truth,' I said, 'I think it could lose twelve minutes.'

I started to move away. He pulled me back.

'Twelve minutes? What the hell kind of crap answer is that?'

'Well . . .'

'I ask you here as a favor, and that's the best you can do? Twelve minutes? It can lose twelve minutes? We're talking about *my job* here, okay?'

He was upset and I had let him down. I suddenly felt

guilty for all the invitations and free Xeroxing this guy had provided for me all those years ago. I could do better than 'twelve minutes,' I was pretty sure.

'Well,' I began, 'not this, but I think it could lose ten minutes in the first half if you just cut out the ex-wife character.'

His face lit up. 'Yes! Of course!'

'And then, I mean, not this, but you could just end it at the kiss in the airport.'

He nodded vigorously. 'I agree. Hey, man, thanks. I owe you, okay?'

He hugged me. I gave my ticket to the valet parking attendant and waited for my car. The truth is, it doesn't really matter where my friend found the twelve minutes to cut. Certain movies can't be too short.

CUT TO:

EXT. TERRORIST CAMP – DAY

Bearded evildoers sit in a circle. One of their number holds a large calendar aloft. A date is circled.

PUSH IN:

He taps the calendar and points to the date.

> EVILDOER
>> Thees, my friends, is the date of our next act
>> of terror!

The group begins to chuckle.

PUSH IN DEEPER:

On the calendar is written in spidery script: 'Premiere of that guy's new sitcom.'

EVILDOER (CONT'D)
> Eeet ees a most perfect date! We will not only
> bring the west to its knees, but we will make
> sure that the premiere of that annoying guy's
> new sitcom is disrupted by news coverage!
> That he never gets a clear shot at garnering
> an audience!

The group chuckle turns into a laugh, then a series of
guffaws, then a crescendo of side-splitting laughter.

DISSOLVE TO:

INT. OVAL OFFICE – DAY

The president is at his desk, surrounded by advisors.

PRESIDENT
> When am I scheduled to deliver my address
> to the nation, outlining my new economic
> and tax policy?

ADVISOR
> We're thinking next Tuesday, sir?

PRESIDENT
> But doesn't that guy's new sitcom premiere
> on Monday?

ADVISOR
> I believe it might, sir.

PRESIDENT
> So then how, exactly, am I going to disrupt
> things by pre-empting primetime program-
> ming on at least one of the coasts, resulting
> in a lopsided premiere and an unreliable set

of initial ratings, thus crushing whatever
momentum his show might have?

ADVISOR

Ummmm. Sir? I'm sorry. Is that one of our
goals?

PRESIDENT

Your goddam right it is. Little shit keeps
talking about moving to France? Not on *my*
watch.

CUT TO:

INT. SOUNDSTAGE – NIGHT

A premiere party is in progress. The cast and crew are
lounging around the set, drinking beer and eating pizza.
We've all gathered together to watch the premiere episode
together. It's been months since we shot it – back then,
before we went to New York and got a series order, we
didn't call it the 'premiere episode.' We just called it 'the
pilot.' But now, barring some kind of terrorist attack or
presidential meddling, it's about to be broadcast coast-
to-coast in primetime.

In years past, we've thrown pretty lavish premiere
parties at swank restaurants and private clubs. There
were self-congratulatory speeches and champagne toasts
and little gift bags and any other act of hubris we could
think of to scuttle our own shaky good luck. This time,
we're playing it cool. Pizza. Beer. A cake. Low key. Head
down.

I'm holding a beer and staring out into the distance.

VOICE (V.O.)
    Hey . . .
ME
    Why does the president hate me?
Our casting director is standing next to me.
CASTING DIRECTOR
    Excuse me?
I snap out of it.
ME
    I'm sorry. I was just daydreaming. Is the show
    about to start?
Our casting director looks at me strangely.
CASTING DIRECTOR
    It *did* start. It's over.
I look around, and suddenly, the sound comes up. Laughter.
The theme music. And applause as the credits roll.
ME
    Great. So now all I have to do is wait for the
    ratings.
CASTING DIRECTOR
    You don't really know how to enjoy a
    moment, do you?
ME
    I've always found 'enjoying the moment' to
    be some kind of trick.
CASTING DIRECTOR
    You're sort of a pessimist, aren't you?
ME
    Give me a break. Is it quote pessimistic

unquote to prepare yourself for bad news?
Bad news that you know is going to come?

CASTING DIRECTOR

Um, yes.

ME

Will you excuse me? I'm going to get another
beer. This one is half-empty.

I cross away.

DISSOLVE TO:

INT. SOUNDSTAGE – LATER

I am standing in a cluster that includes my agent and a
network executive. I have been complaining that the network is ratings-obsessed, and that if we don't do well
tonight, we'll be cancelled quickly, without the opportunity to build an audience. The network executive is trying
to reassure me that this is not the case.

NETWORK EXECUTIVE

Don't focus so much on the ratings.

AGENT

That's what I've been trying to tell him.

NETWORK EXECUTIVE

We look at a lot of things. How much you
retain of the previous show's audience, things
like that.

ME

What else?

NETWORK EXECUTIVE

Oh, you know. It's not all about the numbers.

230

It's about the rating *you* get, the rating the
show *before* you gets, all sorts of stuff.

ME

Like what?

NETWORK EXECUTIVE

Tons of things. Like how many people watch
your show as opposed to how many were
watching *other* shows at the same time. And
how that compares with the show that was
on right before you. Really a whole number
of factors.

ME

Such as?

NETWORK EXECUTIVE

Really just a whole *bunch* of things. We take
loads of things into account. It's not just about
the numbers. It's about *so many* things.

ME

For instance?

NETWORK EXECUTIVE

Well, there's the rating of the show on right
before you . . .

DISSOLVE TO:

INT. SOUNDSTAGE – LATER

I am talking to one of the camera operators and his
wife. He's been on the crew of the last four series we've
done. His wife is telling me how much she likes our
show.

ME

That's very nice of you to say. Thanks.

CAMERA OPERATOR

Really, she really does.

CAMERA OPERATOR'S WIFE

It's true. I remember coming to the pilot
and laughing and laughing and telling him,
*This one, honey, this one is going to be a
big hit.*

ME

Well, from your lips, huh?

CAMERA OPERATOR'S WIFE

And I'm not just saying that. A lot of the shows
he works on are just awful, aren't they honey?

The camera operator shifts uncomfortably. His wife
charges on.

CAMERA OPERATOR'S WIFE (CONT'D)

He was on one show – which one was it,
hon? – and we both just *hated* it, *hated hated*
it. And I would tell him, *Honey, you'd better
be lookin' for a job! 'Cause this one stiiiiii-
iiiiiiinnnnnnkkkkkkkssssssss!* What was the
name of that one?

I silently count to ten, wondering when it will dawn on
her that the show she hated so much was one of ours.

I get to three. Her eyes suddenly widen. She's about to
say something when:

CAMERA OPERATOR

Let's get some more pizza.

He leads her off.

DISSOLVE TO:
EXT. CITY STREETS – NIGHT
I'm driving home. On the hillsides, the lights of a hundred thousand houses glitter like tiny stars. If I look closely, within each twinkle is a flickering blue dot. Each blue dot is a TV. And on each TV is a show.

I wonder whose.

The fairy lights of the hillside are repeated in the windows of the houses I pass, and stacked in neat columns of the apartment buildings and high-rise condominiums that line the Santa Monica freeway.

Flickering dots of blue. Each one a show.

I wonder whose.

CUT TO:
INT. MY BEDROOM – MORNING
It is 5 AM. In one hour, the previous night's Nielsen Overnight Ratings are available.

The 'overnights' are the preliminary numbers culled from the thirty-three major urban television markets in the United States. They tell you how well your show did in the cities. Later in the day, by noon or so, those numbers will be adjusted to include the rural and suburban areas. Those are the 'nationals,' upon which are based things like advertising rates, weekly rankings, and my salary.

The overnights and the nationals can differ widely. A

show that appeals to a primarily urban audience might experience a two or three point drop when the nationals come out; likewise, a family-oriented show might pick up an extra point or two later in the day when the suburban markets are counted.

In fact, there's no real point to the overnights at all, except that when you have a show on the night before, and you're lying awake at 5 AM, you'll take any information you can get.

And also: the first number sets a tone. If it's high, your day is made, a bullet is dodged. If it's low, you wait glumly for the network to send you a fruit basket, to express unconditional support, and then, a few weeks later, to yank you from the schedule. It doesn't really matter that this is just a snapshot. That the number may grow over time, as people find the series and become involved with the characters. That history is paved with the gold networks have earned by sticking with a show they liked despite a lackluster premiere. That the subsequent episodes are funnier, smarter, and more attractive. That this one *has* to work because you're not sure you've got another one in you. That you feel, after a bunch of years in this business and being nice to people and playing fair and doing your best that you're *due*. That you *get it, okay*? That this is a business of set-up-joke-set-up-joke, and this is where the joke comes in, but it would be nice, this time, if the joke *wasn't* on you. You've heard that one already. It's been done a couple of times and we've all had a good laugh but now, really, as you wait for the overnights to come in, you really have to *insist* that we try a *different* joke this time, that the joke be on, oh, you don't know, let's just say the waiter at La Palette, a nice little café on the Rue de Seine, who discovers that the American guy with the idiotic smile on his face is going to be coming in here *every day* from now on, because he lives around the corner and really doesn't have anything better to do than sit on the terrace, sipping a coffee or a *pamplemousse Schweppes* chuckling to himself about network notes, and casting sessions, and phone calls from his agent, and other artifacts of ancient history.

At 6 AM I begin calling the special network ratings phone line. Each network assigns some low-ranking serf to wake up early, collect the primetime ratings for the previous night, and then record them onto a telephone information line, in a voice as chipper as possible.

I call the number. The recording still has the numbers from two days before, which means the new numbers aren't available, or, worse, that the kid has overslept.

I call every five minutes until I hear a new recording.

RECORDED VOICE (V.O.)
> The Nielsen Overnight Ratings for the thirty-
> three metered markets, for Monday, are as
> follows: at eight o'clock—

And I hang up, quickly. This is a fruitless exercise. The numbers that matter, the nationals, won't come out until lunch. The only reason to call in for the overnights is to have something to worry about for the next seven hours.

Whatever. I call the number again.

RECORDED VOICE (V.O.)
     The Nielsen Overnight Ratings for the thirty-
     three metered markets, for Monday, are as
     follows: at eight o'clock—
And I hang up again. It suddenly occurs to me that this
is going to be a long, long set up. I'd better settle in for
the joke.
FADE OUT.

A market research testing facility in Burbank,
California, Friday, 5:15 PM

'How'd we do?'
  'Hard to say, Josh.'
  'What are the overall numbers?'
  'Okay with women eighteen to thirty-five. Better with
men twenty-five to fifty.'
  'Look, Delia's going to be calling me in fifteen min-
utes and I need to know . . .'
  'Delia?'
  'She's the new head of the division.'
  'What happened to Josh?'
  'I'm Josh.'
  'I mean the other Josh. The head of the division.'
  'Resigned.'
  'Resigned?'
  'Well, fired. Delia's the new head. Look, before we call
the writer I need to top line Delia.'
  'Okay. I'm crunching them as fast as I can. Overall

score is not bad. But not much interest in the lead.'

'Damn! I knew it!'

'Some of the other characters are maybe breakouts. People like the agent – especially men eighteen to thirty-five – and they like the setting. Women eighteen to thirty-five like the setting. Older women twenty-five to fifty want more of an emotional story.'

'What about teens and tweens?'

'Not much support with the tweens. A little stronger with the teens. "Too much blah blah" is a typical teen comment from the questionnaires.'

'Okay. Bright spots?'

'Strongly favorable characters – the agent, the various friends – and real eighteen to thirty-five support for the tone and the milieu.'

'Okay. Good. Down sides?'

'Pretty much across the board they don't like the main guy. Teens found him "snotty and uptight." Women eighteen to thirty-five found him unappealing physically and emotionally. Women twenty-five to fifty felt that he needed to grow up. "This guy needs to get slapped" is a typical comment. Men across the board felt he was a complaining candy ass.'

'Okay. Not bad.'

'No, not bad at all. I think you've got yourself a hit. If you lose the guy.'

'Right. Lose the guy.'

'Lose the guy. Everybody wants you to lose the guy.'

'Trouble is, it's about him. I mean, he wrote it.'

238

'So? That doesn't mean you can't dump him.'

'I know.'

'I'm telling you, from these numbers, with him in it, you're dead. Lose him, and you've got a hit.'

'Okay. Okay. That's what I'll tell Delia.'

'Josh? Delia's on line one.'

'Hey! Great news . . . strongly positive. But they want us to lose the guy . . . right . . . just hate him . . . no, just him . . . that's what we're thinking . . . I mean, with him we're dead, without him . . . right . . . right . . . lose the guy, right . . . so do you want to call . . . or . . . yeah, if you think it should come from me . . . right . . . just lose the guy . . . right. Okay. Thanks, Delia. 'Bye.'

'How'd it go?'

'Great. I think she really trusts me with some of the big stuff.'

'So you get to call him and tell him that we're going forward with the project . . .'

'Just not with him in it, yeah.'

'Is that going to be hard?'

'I don't think so. I'll just call him and tell him how the testing went. He'll figure it out.'

'So you're going to call him?'

'Yeah.'

'Do you have his home number?'

'Yeah.'

'So why aren't you calling him right now?'

'Because I think he's home right now. I'll call him later, when he's out.'

ACKNOWLEDGEMENTS

Most of this book appeared in various shapes in several publications, and honesty compels me to admit that some parts of this book appeared more than once. Some of it appeared in print, in print again, and *then* on the radio during my weekly commentary on KCRW, the legendary Los Angeles public radio station. This is called 'repurposing content' in Hollywood, but it's really just another form of laziness and/or fraud. To the various publications – the *Observer*, the *Sunday Telegraph*, the *Wall Street Journal*, *Newsweek International*, the *Los Angeles Times*, the *Irish Times*, and *National Review* – and to the listeners of KCRW, I'm grateful and slightly embarrassed.

Thanks are due to a slew of tolerant editors – Jay Nordlinger at *National Review* and Fareed Zakaria and Mike Meyer at *Newsweek International*, especially – and to Ruth Seymour at KCRW, who have allowed me to work out some of what therapists might call *my issues* on the pages of the magazines they edit and on the airwaves they control. And for money, to boot. Not great money, but still green and spendable.

Also, thanks to my writing and producing partner, Dan Staley, who is far more patient and tolerant than I deserve, and who is such a brilliant writer and savvy producer that it's remarkable he still deigns to work with me.

And to two agents: my former agent, Beth Uffner, who taught me a lot about good sense and the entertainment industry, and to my current agent, Ted Chervin, to whom she taught more.

And mostly to Tim Fall, great and true friend, who read this manuscript several times without once looking bored and irritated, but who surely felt both at times, and who taught me to play golf, and a lot of other things besides.

A NOTE ON THE AUTHOR

Rob Long is a writer and producer in Hollywood. He began his career writing on TV's long-running *Cheers*, and served as co-executive producer in its final season. He has co-written several feature film scripts, including *Just a Shot Away*, currently in pre-production with a France-based production company. He is a contributing editor of *National Review* and *Newsweek International*, and writes occasionally for the *Wall Street Journal*. His weekly radio commentary, 'Martini Shot', can be heard on Los Angeles-based public radio station KCRW, and on-line at KCRW.com. His recent book, *Conversations with My Agent*, chronicled his early career in television.

Rob Long graduated from Yale University in 1987, and spent two years at UCLA School of Film, Theater and Television, where he has also served as an Adjunct Professor of Screenwriting. He serves on the board of directors of My Friend's Place, an agency for homeless teens in Hollywood, and the American Cinema Foundation.

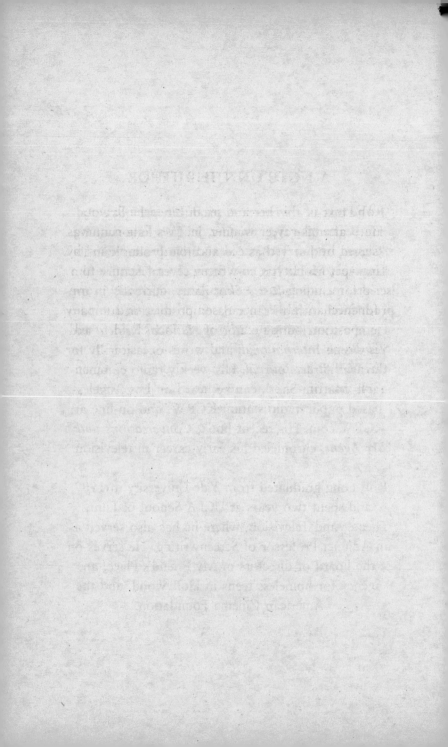

A NOTE ON THE TYPE

The text of this book is set in Linotype Sabon, named after the type founder, Jacques Sabon. It was designed by Jan Tschichold and jointly developed by Linotype, Monotype, and Stempel, in response to a need for a typeface to be available in identical form for mechanical hot metal composition and hand composition using foundry type. Tschichold based his design for Sabon roman on a font engraved by Garamond, and Sabon italic on a font by Granjon. It was first used in 1966 and has proved an enduring modern classic.